La

Carole Morin was born in Glasgow. At sixteen she became a junior diplomat to the United States. She escaped from her first job, as Associate Editor of *Granta* magazine, with the company credit card, and wrote *Lampshades* while suffering from a tubercular toe. She has been writer-in-residence at Wormwood Scrubs prison and Literary Fellow at the University of East Anglia, and noticed striking similarities between the two institutions. (The central heating is never switched off and the inmates are brain-damaging.) She lives in London with Dangerous Donald, a character from her weekly column in the *New Statesman*.

Praise for *Lampshades*

'Original to the point of uniqueness' *Glasgow Herald*

'A bullseye for rotten bad taste' *Observer*

'A purely abhorrent piece of work' *Scotsman*

'Decadent but seductive' *Gay Times*

BY THE SAME AUTHOR IN INDIGO:

Dead Glamorous

CAROLE MORIN

Lampshades

INDIGO

First published in Great Britain 1991 by
Martin Secker & Warburg Limited

This Indigo edition published 1998
Indigo is an imprint of the Cassell Group
Wellington House, 125 Strand, London WC2R 0BB

A catalogue record for this book is
available from the British Library.

ISBN 0 575 40141 9

The Simone Weil quotations are from *Gravity & Grace*
(Routledge, 1952), reprinted with permission from the publisher.

Printed and bound in Great Britain by
Guernsey Press Co. Ltd, Guernsey, Channel Isles

For Don Watson,
a thrill a minute and he has blue eyes

Thanks
to The Author's Foundation,
Hawthornden Castle
and eternally to Engel

CONTENTS

CONTENTS

'Thy will be done'

The Lord's Prayer

BOOK I
Berchtesgaden

'What comes to us from Satan
is our imagination.'

SIMONE WEIL

There are two things: purity and money.

There's only one secret worth keeping: *how to stay clean*.

To be rich is a thrill but to be rich and soiled would be a huge humiliation.

And everyone knows you are better off dead than being dirty and poor.

Purity is power.

The most important thing is not to have a fat brain.

A fat brain goes hand in hand with a weak will.

It can destroy even a thin, white, decisive soul.

But nothing can make you unclean if you retain your spiritual confidence.

That's what I was thinking, lying on the ocean-blue carpet, ear-plugs in, leather sunglasses on, dropping cheap black chocolate from the Stani's between my blood lips, guzzling lemonade. There was a message coming through on my mother's answering machine from an invert jessie biscuit who went to my school. Nylon's voice was muffled beyond Wagner but I knew that he was saying:

Sophira. Hurry up! We're having a fucking ball up here next week. You must come!

This is the beginning, before you started watching me.

When school finished that summer I'd decided not to go out. In the morning I listened for Mother leaving then ran upstairs and vacuumed the sitting-room floor then lay on it wearing my karate suit and my rosary beads with the concealed flick-razor in the crucifix, keeping the remote, her Chinese hand mirror and the tarot cards my grandfather gave me within arm's reach.

The clean cool room is at the top of the house. My dead father's brother Ned painted it pale blue just before he was caught hanging around public toilets hoping for the worst. After that disgrace Mummy scrubbed the room from top to bottom with my beloved blue disinfectant swearing never to speak to Uncle again. She'd been sure he was after her.

Every morning as soon as I was settled I looked up my future on the TV StarStab then went through the tabloids for murder reports. Of course these were the days before the slasher, but there was always something. The best copy is when a child or cat is slaughtered.

As the day progressed I invented long lists in my head of what I want when I'm rich and consulted the tarot every time I felt insecure. Occasionally standing up to practise my favourite kata, Basai Dai, keeping the Teutonic marching music loud, suffering those invitations from Nylon to join him at Balmoral Castle where he's emptying corgi muck for the Queen this season.

On our school trip to Berlin none of the good-looking boys would share a bathroom with Nylon. German bathrooms are spiritually pure. My grandfather Napoleon fought on the Frog side of the Somme, but he loved those Gerries and their clean-living ways. When my brother and I rocked his chair violently back and forth demanding to know why, Napoleon always gave the same answer: 'When you go into a toilet in Germany,' he said, 'you're guaranteed to find it spotless.'

The toilets at Grandfather's house were German thanks to his old slave Gorm. She can't stand other people but she adores disinfectant. She had a large bottle of Blue Dew in her apron pocket every time we stayed at The Haugh.

Grandfather didn't fight in the other war. He couldn't disapprove of a clean well-dressed leader with clear blue eyes and an aura of purity.

Nylon's latest message was rewinding and the phone had started to ring again when Mother breezed in, newly peroxided and wearing an orange sailor-suit with no bra. She has undignified daydreams for a woman that age. She thinks she's Marilyn Monroe! She sold her half of my grandfather's house before he was cold, ruining my fantasy of poisoning her by buying this rabbit hutch in Glasgow which I have no interest in inheriting. She ought to be shot. Tortured first for a long time with a diseased penis belonging to an ethnic minority.

She lunged for the phone before the machine could pick up the call, saying, 'Hi,' in her breathy dial-a-wank voice, prodding me with her ridged vermilion toe.

She crashed the receiver into the cradle shouting, 'Bastard!' then switched my music off and screeched right into my ear: 'Communication from Berlin, Mein Führer.'

'Was that call for me?'

'It was your Uncle Neddie,' she said, pursing her lips in fake disgust. She doesn't give a shite if he has anal sex with five-year-old girls and boys, she's just mad it was in the papers. 'I want to talk to you, Miss.'

She looked at me with her big teeth. My insides surged with renewed relief that I have not inherited her face, body or personality. In fact *absolutely nothing*. We are not even *slightly* alike. She said, 'I sold this house. I am going to India!'

'Why?' I'd rather die than visit a country full of brown things.

'Oh, you know, just *going*. Getting to where it's happening.' She pulled three cleavage shocker cotton tops out of a plastic carrier, holding them alternately against her big body, gazing into the mirror with a letchie smile that betrayed her ludicrous sexual hopes.

'These are the nineties,' I said.

'Yes I know, Miss. And I am going to the home of the wacky baccie!'

'What about me?'

6

'*You!*'

'You can't just abandon me without any money.'

She ignored me, picking up a Chinese vase that reminded me of The Haugh, asking how much I thought she'd get for it. The rage stirred inside me. Staring out the window, I beamed blue fizz at the back of her neck ordering God to make her crumble to dust. – I should have asked you.

'You're sixteen years old!'

'You're about a hundred and twenty-four.'

'Get a job, you skinny little devil, or go to university.'

'Go masturbate,' I said.

She started writing down the contents of the sitting-room on the back of a dating-agency brochure. Glancing up at me she muttered, 'Go live with your Uncle Neddie.'

'Thanks a lot,' I said, gathering up my kit from the floor.

'Don't be silly, he won't touch *you* . . . You're too old.'

She stood at the top of the stairs, watching me climb down to my room, calling, 'Ned wouldn't look twice at you!'

'Sex with an Indian is certain death,' I shouted, slamming my door.

Or was it an African?

Within the week everything was crated and she was fucking off. Even though no one's going to fucking Bombay this fucking year but now that fucking old

7

leftie peroxided tart has fucked off this fucking island I can . . . go to Balmoral Castle and visit Queen Elizabeth!'

At Queen Street Station I bought a brown doughnut and a ticket to Aberdeen and took my seat on the train, eating the doughnut slowly, wanting to stop but having no other way of disposing of the disgusting thing, despising the healthy teenager opposite who was sucking an orange and travelling with *luggage*, trying not to think about Uncle Neddie, whom I have just seen, an appointment that was a degrading last resort – an attempt not to go to this castle where Nylon has promised me free food, a bunk bed and plenty of thrills.

If I'm not there before dark I'll miss the fancy dress contest. *Sophira! Come before sundown*, his last message said, *we need time to get into costume.*

The train was chugging, one of my biker's boots was up on the seat opposite, my sunglasses were on, I was wondering if daft Diana's eyes are bluer than mine, flicking the razor blade out of the arm of Christ dangerously close to the white skin of my throat. I was wearing all-purpose Luftwaffe chic military trousers, (acceptable for sniping, shooting and socialising), SS vest and a starched white cotton shirt (Italian).

The train had been choo-chooing for twenty minutes when it pulled into a siding and just sat there.

None of the other passengers seemed to mind. I was in turmoil about what Neddie said – How dare he, the slimy piece of . . . how dare he even think about my brother never mind . . . – and when we started travelling backwards along the rails I sat clutching the crucifix around my neck thinking, 'It's a sign,' imagining we're backtracking home to Glasgow: city of the chipped shoulder, square sausage and glam razor revival. But next thing I know we're pulling into Perth. The journey's half over.

Off again! Speeding past the maze of brown and green on either side, heading north where houses are made of stone – like The Haugh – skies are reliably glum and the rain is the same colour as the rivers or my dead grandfather's eyes. To help stop thinking about the pervert I was making a list in my head of everything I hate about trains.

Trains in movies are fast and thrilling, full of sensual strangers who drink hot chocolate that never spills wearing solid gold skull-shaped rings with secret poison compartments. But in real life there's this fucking fluorescent light that's never switched off whether you want to have a migraine or not, a non-English-speaking guard who takes a dislike to your feet, a loony who tries to sit next to you and touch your hair, and a fat knackered bastard who moves like a walrus from the expensive understocked buffet back to his seat clutching dribbling polystyrene coffee and a box of jumbo British Rail bacon rolls, blocking the aisle, preventing thin passengers from fetching a bottle of purified water or going to be discreetly sick out of a quiet window that refuses to open. Thank God this is only a four-hour journey.

In the window my gleaming Hitler haircut (rinsed this morning in mineral water) created a perfect outline on the glass.

'You had that haircut when you were young, didn't you?'

Those were Neddie's first words when we met for tea this afternoon on the second floor of the Regal Hotel.

That makes a change. Usually before he's even hauled off his checkered blazer and ordered himself a large selection of stickies he leans his flaking head towards me and mutters, 'It's a bloody disgrace – considering how he felt about them.' He means Napoleon and Women.

The only thing Neddie and I have in common apart from blood is our grievance over Napoleon's will. Grandfather left half shares in The Haugh to Mother and his old servant Gorm. Napoleon hated Gorm and Mother but he hated everyone else more, and I was supposed to be too young. So. Mother flogged her half to Gorm and bought the modern house in the city – which she's now sold to go manhunting in India.

My venom about the suspicious last testament is acceptable but Neddie of course never had a chance of inheriting anything since Napoleon especially couldn't stand pervs and always said of his disappointing son, 'We'll read about him in the papers one day,' long before anything was printed. (According to the *Daily Stab*, Uncle didn't even *pay* the children he molested!)

'That haircut – you had it when you were young?' he said again.

'When I was young,' I lied, 'I had pigtails.'

Of course Donald and I always wore our hair this way. Flicking my fringe into my eyes so that I wouldn't see Ned, I knew already I was wasting my time. I couldn't face living with that. The sight of him makes me retch. It will have to be the castle.

There was a silence. Uncle glowered at me the way loonies who think they're sane look at sane people they think are loonies. He was tugging at one of the folds under his chin. Two ladies came in and sat as far away from us as possible. The waitress took their order before ours.

Eventually I bought a glass of water. Uncle treated himself to four iced pink buns filled with raspberry jam and a pot of scalding tea.

'What're you up to these days?' he demanded, looking around without enthusiasm. During the day The Regal's deserted apart from old gossipy women. At night dressed-up children come in and ask for cocktails.

'Nothing much. Mother's gone to India.'

'Aye,' he said. 'Looking for a man.' He faked a blush.

'Look at that.' He pointed at his chipped front tooth when his mouth was still open from his last bite of raspberry. 'Two guys did that outside the Black Bull . . .'

'Really,' I said, glancing at my beautiful teeth (every one an original) in the window behind his head, 'were these guys dentists?'

He carried on munching and swallowing tea so that the bits of bun in his full openish mouth went soggy. 'This is hot,' he said, screwing up his horrible face every time he slugged.

I gulped down my water and said, 'I have to go . . . there's this train . . .' Looking at my watch, flicking back my hair, standing up.

Out of the blue, as I was turning to walk away forever, he got me.

'You must think about him – now and again.'

'What?'

At first I pretended to myself he meant Napoleon.

'You know . . .' he said, smiling his pervy smile, 'It must be a terrible thing – to outlast your own blood? . . . Your other self, so to speak.'

My throat closed off, the blue fizz welled up, I felt my stomach hardening and my fingers stroking the button on Christ's arm. Uncle opened his mouth to say something else then stopped. Looking away from me, he picked up his cup again, was about to drink, paused then muttered: 'Dead flesh.'

In my head I saw the cup cracking into his face, broken china mashing into the slack skin.

'I'm late,' I said.

'Bye,' he called after me, soon distracted by the arrival of an under-ten with his grandparents.

*

Two middle-aged people on the seat diagonally opposite mine were kissing. Seeing that makes me long to die. It was dark enough now to watch the insides of the train passing outside. But even with my sunglasses on the fluorescents were hurting my eyes. The fool with the luggage was sucking her last orange.

I kept my eyes shut until the train pulled into Aberdeen where there was a black beautiful sky threatening thunder. Shops were starting to close, people were hurrying.

Waiting for the bus to Crathie I spotted Jack Gray crossing the road! He was in fashion at our old school. We called him Mad Jack. Maura McAleer, Irene Munro and Elaine McLean dissolved in tears when he went missing for twenty hours during the school trip to Berlin. He refused to tell the teachers where he'd been.

In the middle of the road he stood still, ignoring the traffic, shook his fringe back and stared right at me. My heart thudded dangerously close to betrayal. I pretended not to recognise him then looked away while he finished crossing. When I looked back the bus to the castle was pulling in and Jack Gray had disappeared.

But you know all this – you know everything – running wild through Europe, time suspended in eternity, hurtling towards your death or glory destiny.

Next time I saw Jack Gray he was sitting in the Balmoral hayloft with his back to the action. The balding brat who fucked up in the marines to go and work in a fucking theatre fucking pink leftie fruit entered the barn and stood on a regal platform watching the gush of servants parading round in fancy dress for him to pick the winner.

Bry Nylon Blomer, the most famous virgin in our old school, who wears off-white nylon knickers, was part of a collaboration of kitchen staff who had gone as Nazis and Jews. He attempted to haul me into the servants' circle each time he passed the corner where I was slouched into the wall, sunglasses on, head pounding, beaming blue fizz to that woman in Bombay, thinking about the River Dee and imagining going there at midnight to dash my head against the rocks in a ruined dive.

'Isn't he the rumpiest?' Nylon giggled. 'Soph, *isn't* he?'

'Jack?'

'*Edward!*' he screeched, before being tugged back into the circle by another of the Jews who were following their SS Guard, a black butler called Bill carrying a tarnished machine-gun.

People can be divided into two classes: fakes and crawlers. But heroes like you know that.

Jack Gray turned, his legs dangling over the edge of the rustic platform. His black boots had been ordered from the same place as mine. He was cleaning behind his fingernails with a gadget attached to the knife on his webbing belt, a determined expression in his pale blue eyes. Bry Nylon had suffered undying love and devotion for him since first year at school, but Jack despised Nylon even more than I did.

He stared me out but couldn't be sure I was looking back because of my glasses.

The balding brat raised his hand and the dressed-up slaves stopped and arranged themselves in a line-up resembling a queue at a urinal. The Queen's favourite failure son jumped from his platform without assistance. He has all the money in the world but it can't bring back his hair. He moved slowly down the line, patted his scalp and pointed at the winner – a tubby chambermaid disguised as a pregnant nun.

He presented her with the prize, which looked like a second-hand toilet brush, stuck his neck forward and poked her with a regal index finger demanding, 'Who *are* you?'

'Alex the Chambermaid, Your Highness.'

'Ho!' Turning to his detective, the Prince murmured, 'Who is he *really?*'

Alex made a thank you speech, in which she said, 'I've been working on this get-up since last year!' It kept her out of the bar, chortle, chuckle. We're all amusing bastards here. We consume *alcohol*. Mein Gott! How fucking amazing.

Nylon and his jessie biscuit fruit friends huddled in a corner consoling Bill the Butler and SS man, whose swollen bottom lip was pouting in the nun's direction because he couldn't blame Edward, the man who would be King if Charles and Wills and Harry and the overweight ex-war hero and his fatneck gabie brats die at sea or somewhere.

Edward praised petted snubbed and giggled with some of the slaves before making a Goodbye speech which closed with the alarming news that we're all leaving the castle for London tomorrow!

While I was reeling with shock Nylon tried to take my picture. I covered my face with my hands.

Jack Gray said, 'Never allow your photograph to be taken. People use it against you later.' Those were his first words to me, though last year at school he had borrowed my German dictionary without asking.

Nylon squealed, 'But Jack you're going to be an actor!'

'That's different,' Jack said, smiling into the distance. 'You can succumb to being immortalised.'

When the dancing started I wandered outside, walking slowly at first, afraid someone would come up behind me and demand to know what I'm doing here and why I'm not a biscuit.

Dancing! Never in my life has anyone been able to make me dance. Even at our birthday parties at The Haugh when Mother tried to force us into something she called the Hoky Poky we ran outside laughing and hid in the trees until it was over. She never followed us into the woods. She stood at the edge screaming with increasing dementia until we appeared, except that one time.

The rain started as I crossed the African-black courtyard past the real house to Nylon's quarters in the tin huts. The long dorm of deserted bunk beds reminded me of Heaven. There's a waiting room there, it's a dormitory, and you have to go to sleep while God decides who's getting to stay forever. – But you must know that.

The toilets with urine puddles and jobbie-clogged drains reminded me of school. I locked myself into a booth, covered everything in tissue, loosened my Luftwaffe trousers, hovered without flesh making contact with the wooden seat, tried to figure out the smell, and was about to start when I was disturbed by two voices.

'Tonight's it . . . Bryan,' the black butler said to my innocent rumpy blond schoolfriend. Nylon giggled ambiguously. My temple, thumping dangerously close to blindness, was pressed against the frazzled wooden door. I could see them entwined by the sinks.

Should I go or stay? I can't face ugliness. Disgusting scenes disturb me for weeks. Looking at Nylon in real life makes me ill. Do I want to see him having his bum buggered by a big blackie jungle bunny through a crack in a toilet door?

Nylon's knickers were at his ankles when I went out. Bill had nothing on. I walked slowly to the exit, asking God to spare me from seeing another bent bare bum for at least the rest of my life.

Every month when she bathed Napoleon Old Gorm would cross herself and say, 'There's nothing worse than a naked man.' She's obviously never seen a naked black man.

Escaping into the trees, encountering no minefields or snipers or jessie biscuit policemen, finding the river easily, climbing a linden in the moonlight, wanting to die there, begging God (still wasting time on Him) not to let me be ugly – *Please God don't let me be ugly, anything but that* – say out loud then laugh, pretend it isn't real. And never to do anything ugly. Never to be unclean. And to have a killer spider and a helicopter and a 9 mm machine gun, and a collection of wigs: escape and evasion kit.

Secretly I also asked for a good destiny and lots of loot and permission to stay in the woods all day shooting cats while singing in haunted soprano. That's not the sort of thing to think out loud. Expect nothing while secretly hoping for victory.

My eyes were soothed by the darkness, my luminous white skin glowed reassuringly, the headache almost went away.

The smell of trees and water and light rain in the blackness reminded me of that last visit to The Haugh with Donald. As soon as we arrived we raced to the bottom of the jungle to our swing in the big linden tree hanging over the sea wall. The medieval moon flicked malevolently through the branches as I worked myself up higher and higher, ignoring Mother calling from the house. Donald sat on the wall throwing bricks at The Stink who was slinking from rock to rock on the beach below. When I swung forward I was dangled over the family vault. When I swung back towards the water my legs made a shadow on the waves.

We spent all our holidays in Grandfather's house in Storm. It kept us out of Mother's hair. Old Gorm let us play outside 'til all hours. Running along the beach to the village while the tide was out, running home to jump on Napoleon's Heaven-white bed or play in the vault because there's nothing to do in Storm. It's been the same for a million years. Donald and I were banned from the sweet shop. Father Batchelor abandoned his opium pipe to run and bolt the chapel door when he saw us coming. We were the indestructible unholy alliance until Don's accident.

There's no chance of me falling from this royal tree into the river – coincidences like that don't happen in real life. Death may repeat itself but lightning never strikes in the same place twice, or whatever it was Old Gorm used to mutter.

When I heard him coming I clutched the rosary tighter ready to press the button for action. But I was hoping it was going to happen. Because that's the exciting thing about death: you never know when. You can plot and imagine but it's out of your hands. Even a suicide can't be sure. Losing control is the ruin of men but embracing the end with passion is power. Uncertainty is poison but loving insecurity is glory.

He shone his crewlight into my eyes and said, 'Your skin's like marble.' We both looked at the flash of white showing at the top of my black boots where my trouser leg had been pushed up by the trunk.

Jack hauled himself into my tree, waking up leaves, climbing higher, telling me it's best being up high, in the tallest branch, more difficult to shoot. Then he sat quiet for seven minutes staring upwards.

'Where did you go that time in Berlin?'

'To see the bunker.' He hesitated. 'They were blitzing it.'

His silence and the black air thrilled me.

'Are you working for the Windsors too?'

'Yes,' Jack said, making a strangling motion, 'I'm the assassin.'

'Who are you going to kill?'

'I came to kidnap Wills, but changed my mind.'

He flicked his fringe back, closed his mad eyes, rested his head on the tree trunk.

'Why?'

'To make me a more disciplined person,' he said, opening the cerulean eyes, staring down at me. 'It was too complicated. And I felt sorry for him . . .'

'Why?'

'He doesn't have any good toys.'

Donald and I had no time for toys.

'His family are fatnecks. They have money but . . .'

'What?'

'They'll always be themselves,' he said, impersonating Charles impersonating a corgi.

He gave a battle-cry and jumped out of our tree, holding out his arms. I climbed down by myself.

We walked through the dead night to the edge of the woods where we could see the house grey and flat against the darkness, like The Haugh approached from the coast, and he pointed out the light in her window.

'It's a fake bedroom,' he said. 'She only goes in there in the morning to shit and shave.'

'Where does she sleep?'

'In the forest,' Jack said seriously. 'It's the most interesting thing about her.' The rain was becoming more obvious. He didn't react.

Not looking at me he asked, 'Are you still sixteen?'

I nodded. Saying it out loud makes me uncomfortable.

'Who did you want to be when you were young?'

'No one.' I was lying. Nefertiti God the Kray twins the Borgia Pope Rebecca (Maxim de Winter's first wife) Caligula Lolita Heathcliff You Son of Sam Dracula Mary Magdalene the usual.

'What about you?'

'Jack the Ripper,' he said, throwing a stone at Queen Elizabeth's window.

It rained harder. The water was dripping from our fringes, first sheltered by the trees then betrayed by them.

'What do you want to do when you leave school?'

'I've left.'

He laughed insanely. The water was running out of us. We're young and dangerous. We don't talk about the weather.

'Let's pretend we're still there . . . what do you want to be?'

'A terrorist. A night-watchman. What do you want to be?'

He leaned closer. His teeth glistened in the dark. I could smell the disinfectant on his breath. He whispered, 'An assassin.' The sound was almost lost in the drip drip of wet wet. When he smiled I was frightened to move.

'Have you seen *Wuthering Heights?*' he asked suddenly.

'Yes.'

'Do you like the bit where the hound gnaws Cathy's leg?'

'I like her death.'

'She couldn't have loved Edgar.'

'She enjoyed Edgar loving her.'

Jack broke off a wet branch with his black leather hand.

'Do you like London?' he asked.

'No.'

'Why not?'

'There are things you can't do in London.'

'Like what?'

'Keep whites white in the wash.'

He laughed, encouraging me.

'Live in a racially pure block.

'Travel on an all-white train.'

'That's impossible here now too,' Jack said. 'But there are things you can do . . .'

He stared right at me, his kiss of death eyes

illuminated and said: 'You look innocent. You could get away with murder.'

Donald and I had always wanted to be assassins. That was my first thought when I woke up in the tin huts at six-thirty by Napoleon's watch, lying in the top bunk with Nylon's feet in my face. His toes were blood red. He had painted them for the party.

Now the heaving dorm of jessie biscuits were sleeping it off and I had another headache. My twenty-second sore head this month.

Old Gorm was an extra in my dream last night. A dream I've never had before in my life. But it made me wake feeling like death, reminding me of my inexcusable secret longing to rewrite the past so that The Haugh doesn't fall into her clutches then I could have died there too. But if I could do that I could change everything.

Last night I lost Jack in the forest and came back here and joined the sleeping jessies and lay awake thinking about how much I hate London.

Jack's going on a mission. He needs an accomplice. Travelling as a team's a better cover. After his mission he'll specialise in deception, become an actor, audition for a part as a hero.

London is dirty. In Glasgow if you stay out late enough you see them scrubbing the streets clean for next day with blue disinfectant, making them smell like the stone stairs at The Haugh.

But Jack's going to be successful. He needs lots of money. And in Glasgow your friends take your success as a personal insult. I want to do nothing. To be rich and safe without undignified effort. Just allow my will to triumph like you did.

We can get a ride to London with the Queen's luggage. It's all arranged. Why doesn't her kit fly with her? Why doesn't it get its own plane? Why doesn't it go British Rail? It drives in a lorry. How common. My head hurts. It's all a bit peculiar but I don't have another idea today; I'll have to go to London in that luggage lorry.

I pulled on my black boots and ran outside. She was in the courtyard disciplining her dogs. Her Venetian silk headscarf flapped in the breeze, forcing me to think about Napoleon who hated Venice where the canal stinks and the natives rumpy-pumpy to music in rotten old rowing boats.

She looked at me sternly and said, 'Stick to the path,' wanting me to disobey so that she can shoot me in the back.

I disappeared into the trees, finding the one from last night at the deserted river's edge hanging right over the water.

I could be happy here alone. Stealing tablet from the estate shop, freezing in the Dee at midnight, sleeping in the castle.

*

The air here is clean and pale like at The Haugh. That last year at The Haugh we were almost seven and Napoleon slept for most of the day, smoking opium in the library after dinner, encouraging us to stay up late.

We kept ourselves to ourselves. During the day in the vault, hiding from daylight with a box of scoff each from the old slave Gorm; or cammed up with warpaint, running through the forest merging with brown and green trees. At night on the beach, jumping across rock pools in the moonlight, shining our torches in dark corners seeking out The Stink, the most disgusting cat in the world.

There were no warnings to be careful, no Bad Men lingering on Napoleon's deserted beach, nothing except the reprimand from Gorm when she caught us at that laughing: 'Stope that laughin' or you'll end up greetin'.' And the slaps she administered after a feed in her kitchen, followed by her demand: 'Whit was that furr?'

'Nothing,' we'd say, fuming blue fizz invisibly through the air from our mouths to hers.

'Keep it that waye,' she replied before lashing out again at our bare legs with her slipper.

Our favourite place was the thorny forest where we buried our dog Wolf beside the stone steps leading underground in the clearing by the sea wall overlooking the spot where James, our father (a man we never met), killed himself. They combed the shore for his bloated body but it wasn't washed up. If it

had been the vault would be full – now that two
more have gone in.

Or maybe not, they may not have let a suicide in –
that last space could still be waiting.

'Too bad his brother didn't follow him,' Napoleon
said after telling us the story on our sixth birthday.

It was in the vault that Donald slit open my hand
with the rosary razor that had belonged to our late
grandmother when she was young. It was kept on a
hook in the library beside all The Haugh keys for
years until Old Gorm had her final run-in with Father
Batchelor, lost respect for God, and gave us the
rosary to play with.

Don licked the red line dripping down my fingers
then I tore his skin and sucked. We pressed our
wounds together and swore never to love another
dog because another dog couldn't be Wolf, another
dog couldn't protect us the way he had until he died
of old age. Then we hid the rosary in the hollow rock
behind Napoleon's father's tomb, and ran up the
steps to our swing.

And when Donald pushed me really hard I
screamed and pretended to go flying over the wall
but the length of the rope and his arms and my own
white legs stopped me. Anyway I can swim.

Once he'd given me a good start Don sat on the
wall, legs dangling insanely over the edge, or stood
throwing pebbles down the spiral staircase, aiming
for the cross on top of grandfather's father's tomb,
while I worked myself up higher and higher, brush-
ing the surrounding treetops.

On Don's last day we woke up in the top bunk squashed into the wall after a bad dream. (But it wasn't about the slasher. He was just little himself in those days.) The morning began strangely: the sky was too black even for us and we picked a bad card and could tell there was to be a fatality later on.

After sharing a bowl of chocolate krispies without milk we put on our green wellies and ran through the trees in pursuit of our enemy The Stink.

Donald said, 'We'll definitely bag him today,' and I nodded solemnly, determined to help even though I dislike touching. Cats slobber over themselves all day long. And any cat owned by Old Gorm is extra foul.

When the tide was far enough out Donald climbed halfway up the big linden using the rope of our swing. Balancing one leg on the sea wall, one against the solid trunk, he hauled me up. My fringe tangled with the frazzled rope. Don tugged it free. We stood staring silently at the water before climbing down on the beach side and picking our way across washed rocks, eyes peeled for the enemy, until we reached the mouth of the vault. We fetched the huge green army-issue spade and the drawstring cat bag that used to house Gorm's clothespegs, and ran up the steps to dry land: ready to track.

Gorm called us for a feed at eleven. We gobbled the moist red meat then mashed up our potatoes and peas and shovelled them into the bin while her back was hunched over the freezer hacking out two equal chunks of white ice-cream for us to swallow down with chocolate pudd. The reeking beast prowled the kitchen while we were eating but scarpered when Gorm went to see why Napoleon was ringing.

Straight afterwards we went back out tracking. We couldn't rest until the unholy cat was bagged. But we were called into the library when Mother turned up unannounced off the afternoon train to sneak in with our birthday presents and pave the way for the man she'd dug up somewhere. Napoleon didn't want to meet him.

'Another disaster,' he muttered, spitting into his fire then working his mouth so that his jaw-bone clicked against the steel plate he'd had fitted after the war. He was shot in the face not by his glorious Gerries but a Frog's own goal. When Mother started one of their arguments we sneaked out of the library window and went straight back to work.

The tide was well in when we pounced on The Stink near the wall. It knew the game was up. Once we had it bagged all we had to do was kick it down the steps to drown in the vault. I undid the drawstring and held the bag open. Donald prodded The Stink's backside with the spade, nudging him closer to Hell.

We hadn't needed to use a weapon on the fat knackered Tom in the Chapel, but The Stink was too quick and sharp for us to fling ourselves on top and squash the daylights out of him. We'd be clawed. Blood sends my heart Whoosh! to the bottom of my right leg. I feel like running a mile. But nobody must ever know. Because the weak are always wrong.

Donald got in two good swipes on the skull before the filthy beast sprang into our tree. I jumped onto the swing, quickly working myself up, unsettling branches, forcing The Stink to dodge. Donald put the big green spade down and climbed onto the wall. He steadied himself then hoisted up the weapon.

As I swung forward into the treetops I lashed at the wicked beast with the toe of my wellington. The mowglie leapt back onto the sea wall, but stopped, refusing to hurtle itself to the drenched rocky beach.

On the backward swing I made a grab with my left arm while Don hoisted up the spade. I swung forward again, willing myself higher, preparing to let go of the rope to dunt The Stink over the edge of the wall to certain death.

Donald stood up, lifting the spade above his head to mash The Stink's brains out. He was ready to slam when Mother's anxious irritated voice called us to Come Quick! On the return swing the sun attacked my eyes. Reaching out to push the cat in Don's direction my bottom slipped and as I fell forward, screaming, The Stink sprang at my brother's throat pushing him backwards headfirst into the rocky water.

He didn't feel a thing. The shock killed him. And of course his skull was smashed. That's what I heard her say later when I sneaked downstairs and stood behind the door listening. She was on the phone to someone stupid and she said, 'Of course it was a terrible blow for Soph – so close to their birthday too,' and I kicked open the big black door and ran in. It swung shut behind me. My breathing was going faster and faster. My head hurt. The first sore head in my whole life. Napoleon hauled himself out of his chair but I reached Mother first and kicked her in the stomach.

'She's sleepwalking,' Mother said and took me back up to the bunk beds and sat there in the dark smoking until convinced I was really in Nod.

Everyone in the house was amazed I was still alive.

First thing next morning I lured The Stink into the kitchen with a dead mouse smothered in chocolate syrup in its dish. I wrapped the rosary round and round my wrist. While The Stink was nibbling I crouched down beside it holding Christ by the legs and pinged the blade out. When I stuck it into its neck I could feel the fur tear. I kept pushing, ignoring the claws and the blood spattering on my white face, concentrating on oblivion and the disgusting brown patches on its coat, until the body went slack. The kitchen floor where we were sitting was slippery with blood and cat flesh. They cook cats in Chinese restaurants.

Suddenly I felt sleepy. My head might've been starting to hurt again too.

The Stink was still breathing but a chunk of its face was missing. The third fingernail on my left hand was frayed.

After a nap I cleansed the kiss of death razor with Blue Dew, polished the beads, and promised to keep the rosary with me forever. Gorm made a fuss about the kitchen floor and having to disinfect the claw mark on my cheek and summon Doctor Feathers. – Doctor said The Stink was going to live, but would be disfigured for the rest of its days.

Death isn't enough for your enemies. It can't recover the loss, cure the broken heart, change the colour of your soul. When time passes you'll forget, it won't hurt as much. That's the worst part.

Gorm never informed Mother that I had slashed her pet cat. Had she already made up her mind to get her own back sneakily, silently, the way ugly old people with nothing else to lose do?

Napoleon died at The Haugh too. Old Gorm was the last person to see him alive. He burned to death on her night off. She was playing bingo in Storm. Mother and I were in Glasgow in our council flat when it happened, but I saw my grandfather's crisped-up carcass on my last trip to The Haugh. He'd been rocking in his chair having a heart attack when the fire started. His name was definitely inscribed in the Book of Death that night. At least he died with his own hair and teeth.

The house was hardly damaged in the fire but Mother said, 'I couldn't ever live here . . . now,' in a stagey whisper.

Old Gorm offered to buy the place. Mother needed money again. The last man she tried to steal escaped without spending a penny and she had me to feed and clothe and her life to use up.

While Napoleon's cronies were whooping it up in the library with Gorm's sandwiches and the last of the opium, Old Gorm fed me chocolate pudd and ice-cream in her kitchen.

When I asked her where she got the money to buy my house she said, 'I've been saving all my days and now's the time to spend it.'

The River Dee is clean. Nobody uses it. It's *her* river. Tabloid photographers crouch behind bushes on the opposite bank hoping a Royal will show itself.

Away in the distance at the edge of the trees I heard Nylon calling me for breakfast, 'Sophira, Sophira!' louder and louder. Jumping to the bank I ran as fast as I could, faster and faster through the forest, pushing branches away from my face.

Were you there already watching over me, ready to make the decisions for me? Was it you who sent me to live in London?

The royal courtyard was filled with an army of frantic jessie biscuits, rushing around bitching and throwing things in crates, loading luggage lorries, lunging in and out of the palace kitchen for advice from Bill the Butler who was seated at the scrubbed wooden table opposite Jack eating fried bread and thick juicy sausages. Jack Gray, schoolboy assassin aspiring actor and billionaire, was feeding on custard marshmallow ice-cream supplied by a sycophantic Crathie dairy desperate for a Royal Appointment sticker for its creamery door. An old man with dandruff sat alone in the corner slurping from a red mug. He nodded to me and said, 'Half an hour.'

Bill said, 'Shut up, Fish.'

Jack asked me, 'Would you like to satisfy your lust for meat?'

'Huh?' I shook my hair out of my eyes.

'Sausage or ice-cream?'

I pointed at his plate. He doled out a large portion for me from a tartan ice-bucket smuggled from *her* table. I still dream about it.

As I lifted the spoon to my lips for my first taste, I asked: 'What's wrong, Bryan?' Nylon was hunched over the sink, tears of pale snot dribbling from the corners of his mad red eyes. He was scouring out the corgi Pooh bowls making them sparkly before the journey home to Buckingham Palace.

'Thinks we're engaged after last night,' Bill said, sucking in his commonwealth cheekbones.

'This is the end,' Nylon said, running into the courtyard crying.

'Someone bit a corgi on the bum,' Bill said, 'and he thinks he's going to get the blame.'

Bill swayed back in his chair, crossing his legs, and pulled a wad of prints out of his pocket. 'Chas and Andy,' he said, 'really camp stuff – yours for five pounds each.'

My mouth was full of ice-cream. The butler interpreted this as interest.

'I'll give you a complete set for fifty pounds.'

'I don't have fifty.'

'How much have you got?'

I shrugged. Jack stood up and walked to the refrigerator. He cracked open a can of lemonade then sat back down watching it de-fizz in a crystal glass.

The old man in the corner suddenly put his mug down and stood up. 'Half an hour,' he said, 'and anyone not ready gets left behind.' He walked over to us, chapped the table with his knuckles and asked, 'Do any of you need to go?'

'Yeah,' Jack said.

The old man's third finger has an extra broad joint and a fifties band of gold. Men his age are always married, but he's left-handed as well.

'Well then,' he said.

'Well,' Jack said, baffled.

'As you please,' the old man said, 'but this is a straight run. There will be *no* stops for number ones or number twos. Understood?'

'Yeah,' Jack nodded.

The old guy went to slash. Jack and I fell on the floor laughing. Bill said, 'Fish is driving you to London . . . nothing to laugh about, honey. I'*m* travelling with Her Majesty. You guys are going with the corgi luggage.'

I hate London. I can't live there with off-white underwear and jungle-bunny neighbours and polluted water and rats getting under my feet.

Jack stood up. His profile is perfect. The sort of face that doesn't have trouble making decisions. He said, 'If I don't get more ice-cream I'll kill the hostages.'

'Do you live in Buckingham Palace?' I asked Bill.

'Yes, honey,' Bill said, 'me and Her Majesty and the rest of the Queens, but don't get your envy up. It's like a disused public toilet.'

That's when I had my idea.

The courtyard was still cluttered with millions of disorganised slaves. Nylon was trying to round up the dogs. In half an hour everyone would be gone. Twenty minutes. If I could just be alone I'd think up an infallible way of staying here forever with all the mud and trees.

And no one will disturb me if I lock myself in QEII's toilet! Because I can't go to London. Something bad will happen there.

The old man came up to me and asked, 'Have you been yet? This is your last chance.'

'I'm going now.'

Entering the house was easy. There was no guard on the royal door. The rosary pressing against my flesh under my shirt was comforting.

The royal corridor leading to her rooms has frayed tartan carpets with stray flecks of corgi muck. I didn't set eyes on a soul, but kept my hand on Christ just in case.

From the big gloomy window in Elizabeth's room I saw Nylon packing dog kit into Fish's green truck. Fifteen minutes left by Napoleon's watch.

I sat down on her royal blue bed. It's embarrassingly big for one body and has the same unlived-in smell as Napoleon's massive four poster at The Haugh. He was always asleep in his chair in the library, he didn't need the canopied tomb watched over by a lifesize portrait of the real Napoleon.

QEII shares her room with a painting of herself when she was young. And in the morning Bill comes in to light her fire, because in summers in Scotland there's always a draught, and Bill reminds her of the Commonwealth and the way things were when Queens were Queens and men were men and Queens scared men shitless with the threat of decapitation.

Ten minutes to go. Seven?

No chance of finding a thousand pairs of diamond encrusted stilettos under her bed, but I had a quick look anyway then went into the bathroom.

She was sitting on her toi, her profile to me. The reflection in the mirror revealed an expression I haven't seen on her face before and a rusty chain dangling behind her head. The famous hairstyle was concealed under a blue travelling hat.

The commode was low. The type with dangerously high water, so that even if you're the sort of fool to sink your bum right into the seat you wouldn't do that on this toilet because the water might brush your flesh. She was squatting slackly, knees wide. Her eyes were open though she looked blind. But as I tried to back noiselessly away, she said, 'Wash your hands then give me a dose of those . . .'

In the mirror I could see a bottle of brown laxatives with the top off sitting on the cistern behind her head. She was near enough to reach herself.

'Hurry up,' she said, muttering under her breath, 'you people are a waste of rations.'

I rinsed my fingers under the hot tap without touching her soap. It smelled like death. It would be ideal to perfume the insides of a satin-lined coffin.

You can never be sure about someone else's towel so I reached for a bit of toilet tissue. Her foot was in the way. I stubbed my boot against her electric-blue slippers and held on to the roller too long, dragging off the last piece of white paper.

'Careful you fool,' she said, trying to kick me in the shin. My razor was ready and waiting round my neck. What would happen if she started something?

'Damn,' she muttered to herself. 'It could put you off for life.' Her face was barely recognisable. The eyes were scrunched, the tongue lolling to the left.

I moved forward and emptied two pills into her gnawed hand. There was something yellowish-cream crawling up the wall next to the toi roller. I had to fight to stop myself visualising it making a home in her pubic hair.

She saw me staring and reached out her hand impatiently mashing the louse into the tiles.

'That's all,' she said, shooing me away. I stared at

the corpse flattened against the wall until a new smell infused the air.

As I backed away into the bedroom she shouted, 'Wait a minute, I need another roll of paper – better make it two.'

'Yes, Your Highness.'

'Hurry up!' she said wearily. I looked at Napoleon's watch. Three minutes left, but it's always fast. Outside the courtyard was quiet. The slaves were gone. The luggage lorries had disappeared except for Fish's truck.

She let out a fake middle-aged orgasmic yell and an extra strong pong filtered out and I ran like mad along the royal corridors, downstairs, outside, spitting out big gulps of stale air in the courtyard.

The old man revved the getaway truck, Jack held open the door, going against the feeling of doom inside I jumped in. Jack said, 'I was just about to shoot the hostages,' and we drove to London.

BOOK II
Triumph of the Will

Part One

Rastenburg

'When I am in any place
I disturb the silence of heaven . . .
by my breathing
and the beating of my heart.'

SIMONE WEIL

It's Tuesday again and I'm devouring the breakfast sacrifice, sitting on one of the sea-blue couches in reception sheltered behind the *Daily Stab*, studying an identikit photofit of the slasher who claimed another soul last night. The jelly babies are making me thirsty. I could cross the street to the Stani's for a can of lemonade, but standing up will make my head worse and the dirt in that shop depresses me.

At least it's clean here in the Royal Hotel. Clean*ish*. Most of the staff are white. The food is English. The colonial columns fronting the portico recall our glorious slave-owning past.

Last night I couldn't sleep again. This time I followed Jack.

After lights out, tucked tightly the way I insist under the ice-starched cotton sheets, I could see the silhouettes of our crystal lemonade glasses glistening in the dark on the table between my bed and his. Because of my sore heads in the middle of the night I feel insecure without a drink nearby.

As I lay staring at the bright glass the smell of antiseptic wafted through the dark then the sound of his razor scratching across the stone. Sharpening stones remind me of Mother. She always attacked her big feet with one before the first rumpy-pumpy with a new man she was trying to steal.

I waited for Jack to leave then threw my leather jacket and his jeans on and went after him.

Outside the air was transparent black. The streets were dead. He became visible on the other side of the road dressed in his Third Reich casuals, moving innocently but quickly with the Bergen packed with sand on his back.

'Get motivated,' he keeps telling me.

How?

'Run, get yourself a pack.'

The SS trained with loads of dead Jews but that upsets people these days. Bill the Butler had given us permission to steal Jack's sand from Buckingham Palace courtyard one night last week. I had shone the torch while Jack shovelled the sand into his pack. What if it has beasts in it?

He's using it to strengthen his will. He doesn't fear insect life.

It was only half-past twelve. Napoleon used to say, 'Women out after midnight deserve what they get.' His soul was more German than anything else, but you of all people know that.

A nosy parker who'd lost his dog came charging out of Hyde Park and asked Jack where it had gone. Jack shrugged. He crossed Park Lane without looking back then dodged into Bishop Place, a dead-end street with a closed cemetery. The man without the dog stared after him. Anyone over forty out after midnight without a dog on this island has had it.

Running, the wind on my cheeks, I lunged across the road ignoring the midnight traffic, going faster and faster until I reached the locked gates. No matter how quick I move I can always imagine it quicker.

Climbing the broken Catholic railings I caught my reflection in a puddle then tiptoed across a path of sunken graves, eyes peeled, trying not to inhale or touch the breathy blue flowers between the flat stones with my wee feet.

Death fever is engrossing at night. This island has a death culture. Dead poets beat hell out of living geniuses, dead beauties excite our souls, your own death is the unspoken terror, only mentioned as an occasional throwaway joke.

My head was sore again. It could hurt for the rest of my life. Mother used to say, 'It's your guilty conscience.'

Silence thrills me and the graves soothed me. My luminous face and hands lit the dark and I willed Jack Gray to see me and jump out from behind a stone.

Catching sight of my reflection in the stained glass wall of the abandoned chapel, suddenly he was standing beside me taking a picture of a marble tomb with a glowing eagle on top. His Bergen was balanced against a moss-covered headstone. He had removed one of his gloves and stuffed it into the front pouch of his webbing belt. The flash on his Praktica camera stabbed my eyes. I didn't know he had a camera. He's full of surprises.

'Sophira,' he said, 'so nice to see you.' He pointed the machine, shooting me with light.

We stood side by side staring at the grave.

'They must have really loved each other . . .'

He meant the two names on the tombstone. It's a fresh grave. The dead German Dr Jürgen Riefenstahl was buried just after the war, but joined recently by his frau Magda.

'Who are they?'

Jack shrugged. 'I like the eagle.'

'Have you ever known anyone who died?'

'No,' he replied, touching me with his gloved hand, 'but I'm just about to.'

He flicked his razor open, making the sign of the cross on my forehead. The shiny metal was cold but calming and definitely clean.

'Me?' My razor was round my neck with the safety-catch off.

'Death for betrayal,' he said, laughing his mad laugh. 'Did you see that movie?'

'What movie?'

'The one about vengeance.'

'No. What's it called?'

'The one I'm going to be in . . . I just made that up.'

He laughed harder, running away from me, trampling blue flowers, dodging behind upright stones, the insane noise echoing. He vanished in the mist.

I walked back here to the hotel slowly and lay on top of the covers until morning, willing the headache throbbing above my eye to go away.

Jack doesn't believe in headaches. His formula for murdering them is a command to chew on the right side only. It still feels strange, but it works. If I chomp my left jaw the throbbing above that eye becomes unbearable; and I can't have my bath yet. Taking a marble bath locked in the cave bathroom forces pain away. But the maid's still cleaning our room.

Staring at the tabloid picture of the slasher (the papers say he's mad), I was engrossed in his kiss of death eyes when P. D. Hose, the evil blond banana who manages this hotel, leaned over my paper and whispered, 'Would you like a copy of your bill *so far*?'

I smiled, folding the print-out he gave me and placing it in my breast pocket. He smiled back. Like the American actor picked to play the villain, Mr Hose has badly aligned teeth. In real life in London it's easy to distrust men with foul breath. But Mr Hose obviously doesn't trust us. Anyone under thirty is suspicious in this country, especially when they book an indefinite stay in the Royal Hotel. Anyone under twenty has had it.

Hosie is right about me. I don't have a penny. When Jack gets back he has to have money. He should be here by now. He's usually in the room when I wake.

Hose peered at my paper, smiling a pervy smile that reminded me.

'They haven't caught him.'

'No,' I said, shutting the *Stab* and tossing it under the table like I didn't want it. It's yesterday's. Jack brought it in with him. This morning I discovered a chunk missing from page thirteen.

'Ah well,' Hose said, 'at least he doesn't rape 'em.'

When he left me in peace I picked up the paper and removed the mutilated page. On one side there were advertisements for cheap slaves, on the other film news.

Cussons, the assistant manager (28, 5' 11", natural black hair, small eyes), was watching me from the desk. He couldn't tell if I was looking back. He has one of those faces that's almost good-looking; it's impossible to decide why it isn't.

One of the room-service waitresses approached him from behind and put her fingers over his eyes. He shrugged her off, laughing. He's married. Mother used to say, 'There's nothing worse than a married man who's cheerful.'

Mein Gott. The room must be clean by now. Jack will be back soon. I need first bath.

Waiting for the automatic lift I studied my brilliant white face in the glass doors. The chandelier above my head caught the glisten of the inherited sapphire ear-rings on my small white ears. Cussons was staring at my back. He was wearing a macaroon casual under his uniform. I dislike silly colours.

Travelling upwards pressed against middle-aged middle-class gut-buckets turned my stomach, but I can't run up the stairs with a blinding head.

At the first floor I stepped out of the lift. The fat noise closest to me said, 'Beware of the slasher.' The other buckets laughed.

The working-class blonde cleaner was still fiddling about in our room. That woman's hair's a wig. If I didn't know it was impossible I'd suspect her of snooping through our kit. But I keep the interesting stuff in my pockets, and Jack takes his Bergen with him every time he goes out.

I kept on walking, as if I was really going to some other room, and stopped at the end of the hall, sitting down on the ice-blue cushioned window seat. Outside it was raining. I love Tuesdays. Tuesdays and Thursdays are my best days.

Fat men in big dripping cars cruised the busy street, passing the discreet massage parlour and the

Stani newsagents and the synagogue which chimes the hours away.

A man with a familiar head stopped longingly at the entrance to the Palace Parlour. He wasn't wearing a hat. His thinning fair hair was damp from the rain. He felt me watching him and looked up. My insides stiffened but I didn't move – I knew it couldn't really be theatrical Ted, the fancy-dress judge. I stared down the street purposefully in the opposite direction.

Newsprint from the mutilated page contaminated my hand as I admired the rain drizzling down the big gloomy window, pulling the zip of my jacket up and down. What did he cut out?

The bald blonde moved next door but I sat on at the window to make it look natural. She bustled in and out of the neighbouring room emptying the bathroom trash, the bedroom trash, the miscellaneous trash, into one of her black sacks. We've never seen the face of the guy in there but he sleeps alone, has round shoulders . . . and reads the *Daily Stab*!

A baby was wheeled past. The maid smiled at it. The tyres of its pram ran over the corner of one of her binbags.

'Excuse me,' I said, beginning my rehearsed speech. 'I'm from room 100.' I held out my key, gave her an honest smile. 'I think I lost something . . . could I take a look through your trash?'

She was wearing a *Chrissie* badge on her right melon. Her mouth was set stiffly like it had just been forced into a rare bout of oral sex. Her apron had seen better days. She obviously has plenty of time at night, why doesn't she starch it?

But it must be uncomfortable being bald and having to wear a tight yellow wig and work as a cleaner with a pattern on your forehead when you're that age. Poor people past thirty are an eyesore. Someone should slash her brains out.

'Go ahead,' she said. Really she didn't want me rummaging, but didn't like to say No. She's a different breed of servant from Old Gorm.

I waited until her back was turned then grabbed the *Stab* and locked myself into our bathroom and sat on the cold tile floor, shining Jack's crewlight on page thirteen. The *Daily Stab*'s astrologer StarStab is available for intimate consultations costing fifty pounds. Investing fifty pounds in my future could be a thrill.

You're mentioned in a small paragraph near the bottom on the other side of the page. They're making a movie about you, beloved Adolf, a true biopic of your life! Your story's worth telling. You're the star of eternity, the only actor worth watching. We all secretly want to be you.

I tore the interesting bit out and hid it in the lining of my biker's jacket then turned the taps on full blast to fill the big marble bath to drowning depth. The naked bodies of millions of people have been in this bath but it has just been scrubbed by Chrissie and rinsed by me. Bathing in the dark purifies the soul.

There's no window in the bathroom attached to our room (all the worse for peeping Toms, Jack says) and no light. But big bright lights annoy me and Jack's allocated me his spare torch (all the better for discreet seeing).

Usually I take two unlit baths a day, sometimes three, bolting the door, emptying in a bottle of blue disinfectant, having my razor crucifix ready on the edge of the cracked marble tub on the other side from the soap.

It's best to be prepared. The slasher could be coming. The slasher could be Jack. We all know that.

Successful egomaniacs make excellent murderers. Boys with mein kampf stares and kiss of death intentions. His white innocent face and clever eyes and brave mouth and long fingernails ready to draw blood. The killer smile, the determined soul. Obligatory mad laugh like an actor imitating passion.

I unzipped my leather jacket and stepped out of Jack's jeans. I have gained a pound. It's on my left buttock. I hid my body under the fizzing blue water.

George VI banned mirrors in his castle. He couldn't stand the sight of himself. I have always hated looking too, but I have to examine my face. Steeling to do it is easier than suddenly catching a disappointing sight of it in the window of the Palace Parlour when I'm hurrying out of the Stani's with my supply.

Switching the crewlight onto full beam I wiped the mist off my magnifying mirror and saw the familiar crack on my left fang, the broken strand of hair at the peak of my hairline, a new piece of dead skin on my lower lip.

The right cheek was glistening alabaster perfection.

But on the left cheek I saw a blemish off in the distance possibly attempting to surface near my mouth as a faint faraway line. But it wasn't a broken blood vessel! Mein Gott, people with those should shoot themselves or at least have the decency not to appear in public. This little mark on my face was the sort of thing that can be obliterated by will.

Control your face.

After adoring your reflection you measure other faces against your own. They are either too old or too young depending on how far away they are from you. If you fall madly in love the other person is either a more perfect version of you or impossibly unlike you.

I switched off the beam, recharging the batteries, taking a break before tackling the rest. Any minute Jack's sure to come in and switch Wagner on. He could be downstairs in reception now drinking lemonade. We're addicted to fizzy pop and jelly babies. He's always back by this time.

Reclining in glorious silence, allowing the bathwater to de-fizz, I flicked the torch back on and held the mirror at my nose then chin. Nothing. Still uncorrupted. In celebration I sloshed more Blue Dew into the water. Did you ever see that advert? A blonde in a white bathrobe floats into her steamy white-tiled bathroom, reveals her bare back, and breathes, 'Add a little . . . Blue Dew to your bath.' That commercial was banned when I was young but blue disinfectant's still sold as a bleach. It leaves me stinging with cleanliness.

*

At first the mark on my left temple looked like a shadow. Then I pretended it was a stain on the glass. I touched it and felt a bump. When I held the mirror closer I saw two tiny crosses etched in blood just above the eyebrow. Intricate three-dimensional cuts slashed into the shape of a twin crucifix.

My heart went Whoosh! to the bottom of my right leg and I jumped from the bath and ran dripping into the other room. At the window I pulled open the blue velvet curtains. Jack insists on them being closed even though the balcony protects us from the busy street below.

'You never know who's watching,' he said. And he was right.

I examined my head again. The bloody marks were still there growing dangerously close to my left eye. If my fringe was any shorter it wouldn't come down far enough to cover them.

Have they been caused by the headaches? Will they grow and grow? Take over my whole face? Blind me? Make me ugly!

They're stigmata! I'm a chosen one. My fate is sealed.

But in this light my brilliant blue eyes are grey-blue. The stigmata eye doesn't seem less blue than the right eye. I looked away from the mirror out the window then back again quickly. Nothing's changed.

Controlling my reckless heart I put the mirror down and stared straight ahead. What can I do? Climb out onto the balcony and jump? Mein Gott, what if this growth spreads? What if anyone mentions it?

I looked at the inseparable red crosses again. They're quite nice. Don't let Jack Gray see. Make sure he doesn't.

When the synagogue bells chimed three times I saw Jack down in the street talking to an especially fat man. (Am I imagining it? How long have I been standing at this window?)

They finished their dialogue and the fat man climbed into the front seat of a long black car. He's driving himself. He's all alone in his expensive machine.

Jack turned. I crouched down on the faded blue carpet and peered at him through the spars of the balcony. He disappeared into the Stani shop.

I pulled on his jeans and my starched white Italian shirt and sat on the bed opposite the TV, sound down, applying blood to my lips. When he comes in I must act normal. Convince him there's nothing different about me.

He'll have bought his paper by now and some babies, he'll be crossing the road. He knows how to cross a road. Any minute now he'll come into the room and not mention last night. He must be in reception waiting for the key. They'll tell him they don't have it, he'll know I'm up here.

There's a game show on telly. I flicked it round to a programme about snakes having sex, then a re-run of a seventies situation comedy, keeping the sound

off because I don't want him to think I'm watching.
The only one not chortling was me. The only funny
thing I have ever seen on television in my whole life
was the night before my German exam when Tommy
Cooper died laughing onstage and the audience
thought it was a joke. His body was dragged behind
the curtain. All the news bulletins that day and the
next screened action replays. Commentators said:
'He would have wanted it this way.'

Nylon, the first kid in my class to own a video,
had it taped. Maybe I should go visit him at Buckingham Palace?

Half an hour later Jack still wasn't in. He could have
got stuck in the lift? He never uses the lift. He takes
the stairs. He could be talking to someone in
reception?

He must have gone back out again. I took the
magnifying mirror from the bedside drawer and
sneaked another look. The stigmata were still there
but the blemish that was beginning on my left cheek
had disappeared. I lay down flat, arms folded across
my chest, and willed the cross to go away. There's a
headache pounding in the distance, getting closer.
The headaches must be to blame for this growth.

Breathing, lying still, willing my eyes to be bluer
and my face to stay alabaster forever, I started
daydreaming about the slasher again: imagining the
colour of his eyes (blue of course), his smile, how his
nails must smell.

There's a theory that you're always murdered by a

man you know; and another that raving loony psychos never hurt the one they love. But I am safe. I have sworn the Oath of Loyalty, promised bravery until death, my rosary is round my neck.

What do I want from life? What are my plans for the next ten years? The slasher doesn't ask these questions. He doesn't lie on his back staring up at the dusty art deco electric chandelier wondering whether to put on some music. Music uplifts the spirit. Purifies the soul. Forces decisions.

Maybe I should kill someone, just once, to see what it's like. My Indian mother, Jack, a child in the street.

To make me a more interesting person. For spiritual profit. For power and glory. Financial gain? Nothing.

The only murderers who get caught are the chatterboxes. There are millions of unsolved slaughters committed by people who only did it once, became more interesting, then zipped their mouths.

I jumped off the bed, shook my hair back, applied more blood to my lips and ran across the street for the latest on the mad one. He's made the front page. The police have a number of leads but no suspects. They feel certain they're close to catching this depraved sex monster who doesn't rape his victims. But they can't give details. But they're definitely hot on his trail, after his blood, ready (almost) to pounce.

The composite picture of the flick-knife phantom has been blown up to poster size. He'll be advertised across London, all over the country. He could be in Berlin. He might be in Bavaria. The police are leaving no stone unturned. They're doing an excellent job tracking this bloodthirsty beast.

Their sketch of him is nothing like how he really looks. While I was studying the picture, comparing it with the one in my head, Jack came in. He threw his gloves and a bunch of ancient blue flowers down on his bed and went into the bathroom leaving the door open. He doesn't look as if he's just pegged someone out. His face is young and clean. It changes regularly. Back and forth it goes from old man to little boy. He's looking at himself in the mirror. He flicks open his blade, holds it to his throat, laughs. Turns on the taps, rinses the steel, dries it on the white hotel towel, snaps it shut, puts it in the pocket of his combat shirt, calls through to me:

'Blood for Dracula?'

'Huh?'

'Let's go down to dinner.'

Something unpleasant interrupted dessert.

Jack and I were seated in our corner table with a view out the window of middle-aged middle-class soft-bellied men going into the Palace Parlour for a discreet massage.

The red glass lamps on each table were lit, except those tables with dead bulbs or no one sitting at them. The hunchback waiter drew the blue velvet curtains, and I sat with my back to the corner watching the other tables and a vision of myself in the big baroque mirror.

The dining-room's half empty but smells as if it's full. Jack said an illegal immigrant defecated under the corner table five years ago and the brown blob's still fermenting undisturbed near the feet of the blocked-nose jungle bunny who's sitting there smiling now.

'Why didn't he go to the bathroom?'

'Who?'

'The immigrant.'

'They have no self-control.'

Staying in control is the most important thing. Murderers only get caught because they can't restrain themselves. They don't stop on time. But disciplined killers definitely become stronger braver people.

The hunchback dwarf waiter who doubles up as night-porter dumped our liver down, splashing the white cloth with clogged blood, then shuffled off pretending he didn't hear when Jack requested a napkin. He has a job serving everybody at once.

Chomping half-heartedly on animal organ, strictly adhering to the rule and using only the one side of my molars, I couldn't take my eyes off the waiter's hump. It looked like it was sewn on. And he's a man who delights in his misfortune. Without warning he spun round from his serving-trolley specially to catch us speculating. Jack stared him out I lowered my eyes to study my scoff. There were crumbs stuck to the edge of the damp plate, the remains of someone else's dinner.

All through the blood course I was longing for a toi. Should I go back up to our room or risk the one down here?

The key to room 100 was resting on top of Jack's Bergen which was leaning against the back of his chair. The hunchback sneaked by and tried to move Bergie while Jack was hacking off a piece of bread. The dwarf was dragging it towards the exit – carrying it on his shoulders being out of the question – when Jack, who has eyes in the back of his head, stood up and shouted, 'Leave that.'

The Americans at the next table put down their forks. The hunchback continued to haul Jack's pack between the tables.

Jack tugged it away from him. The dwarf was mad.

When he brought our chocolate pudd he thudded the glass bowls down causing brown gobs to squirt onto the cloth beside the bloodstains.

'Wipe that,' Jack said. Slop irritates him. The dwarf's pretence at deafness reminded me of Old Gorm. He'd make a suitable husband for her if she wanted to share The Haugh. Still, it can't be easy being over forty and a dwarf and working nights in a hotel managed by a man who resembles an overripe banana.

'The death warrant is signed.'

My stigmata were itching. I put my hand up to cover them, stopped myself, pushed my fringe into my eyes.

'Some people sign their own death warrants.'

'Huh?'

He didn't answer. He was staring at the dwarf.

During the fracas the key to our room had slid into the pouch at the top of Jack's bag. Now if I wanted to go to our toi I'd have to reach over and put my hand in to remove the key. Jack would be disturbed. Naturally he'd wonder why I had to go to the room. He'd be surprised that it – whatever it was – couldn't wait until after dinner.

Why can't I wait? Why can't I just wait until he goes out?

Scoff was almost over but my insides were stiff and ready. I couldn't force myself to swallow another mouthful of chocolate pudd. My heart wasn't in it. My fantasy about the closest toi was devouring me.

I imagined myself escaping from here and passing reception without having to make eye contact with Cussons, slinking into the corridor to the left of the lift then getting into the toi and finishing without being disturbed.

But would there be women in there at this time of night? Surely not, they'll all be out rumpy-pumpying, or locked into the bathrooms attached to their rooms.

Jack asked me if I was OK. I nodded. Then he said, 'Never forget your destiny.' It seemed sudden, but he'd obviously been discussing destiny while I was in torment. The big gold mirror revealed nothing of my despair. The pale confident face broken by two hard dots and framed with dark hair was safe beside the back of Jack's perfect head.

Suddenly I stood up. People do forget their destiny. That's what's wrong with them. They're afraid. You never forgot yours. You changed this century more than God. You left a mark no one can erase. Your enemies give you eternal life with each denunciation.

'Excuse me,' I said to Jack. Only a moment before I would have invented an excuse to visit our room – a forgotten sapphire, an imaginary phone call, a bath left running. But I stood up and made my dramatic exit with my head high dreaming a destiny like yours. (That's the mistake.)

It wasn't until I had successfully marched along the corridor without meeting a soul and bolted myself into the small ice-blue toi that I noticed the unflushed jobbie.

Sometimes when I enter a new toi – pushing the door open slowly, jumping in quickly – suddenly it's Sunday! But that night I felt like I was in another country. Holding my breath I leaned over to check the seat and was confronted with that *thing* floating. As soon as I saw it I went dizzy and imagined a claustrophobic smell and felt wretched about anal sex and couldn't wait to get out of there – but there was someone outside! A middle-aged Englishwoman's swollen knuckles tapped on the blue door.

'Are you going to be long in there?' she shouted in a voice used to getting its own way.

Mein Gott, she's beyond funny. I've been in here seconds. I flushed the toilet. Why has God done this to us? He could easily have used a more dignified design for the body. Why does there have to be this fucking little room called a *toilet*? When you go into a toilet *everyone* knows *why* you're in there. They know what you are going to do sitting on the plastic seat with your underwear lowered. They have a rough idea what it will smell like and an expectation of how long it will take. It's inevitable, it's death.

The selfish bitch rapped on the door again. I was afraid to look down the bowl in case the second-hand jobbie hadn't flushed away.

What will I do if it's still sitting there?

If I go out and leave it this sagging English frump will assume it's mine. She might complain to P. D. Hose. I wouldn't have minded taking the blame so much if it had been my own. At least when it's one of yours you have an idea what it's made of and that it's quite clean. You can look it in the face if you have to. Mother always insisted on us checking colour and shape. I avoid looking now, though sometimes when I see it accidentally I can't help being impressed.

But that woman's out there trying to get in and I still have one to do! She'll probably break the door in.

'What's going on in there?' the voice asked.

Mein Gott, how dare she! But she wasn't asking me. She had been joined by a west-coast American. There was now a queue of incontinent middle-aged women forming to use this soiled toilet. I could feel their impatient breaths and the unspoken question forming between them: Does the girl in there inconveniencing us have constipation or diarrhoea?

I'd completely gone off the idea of doing one. It would take me ages, there might even be blood as it cut its way free, and – when it came – they would hear the plop. So I flushed the toi again and steeled myself to look. Miraculously the thing was gone.

When you depart from a toi leave no evidence you've been there. Impossible when you're seen coming out.

The new woman barged past the Englishwoman saying, 'You don't mind if I go first?'

I hurried back without washing my hands. The hunchback was alone in the dining-room, standing on top of his serving-trolley stashing half-eaten cakes in a concealed cupboard halfway up the wall. The crystal bowls flecked with mushy brown pudd were still on our table. Jack hadn't finished his either.

That dinner was the last time I saw Jack until his picture started appearing in the papers.

When I went up to our room he was asleep with the blue cover pulled up over his head. He takes sudden naps to compensate for the all-night photography forays.

In the bathroom mirror I noticed a scarlet smudge on my Dracula teeth. It looked like I'd been chewing blood.

I took another bath, sprayed myself in Blue Dew, checked the stigmata in torchlight then climbed into my bed certain the growth's no bigger than it was this afternoon. Quite cheerful, maybe.

*

For once I fell asleep straight away.

A brilliant white woman is lying naked on the damp black grass in the cemetery, legs parted, holding her round red heart in her hand, looking up at him with open blue eyes, moist ruby lips, ice-white hair sprawled behind like a Nun's veil. The wounds on her luminous flesh look like criss-cross kisses in the moonlight.

He snaps his razor shut. There's a spade propped against the linden tree behind him. The woman's ice-cream grave is rippling open.

'Sophira,' he says. 'How nice to see you. How are you?'

Jack comes slowly towards me. In a minute I could be in his arms forever. He leans in close, presses the jagged silver against my face, carving stigmata out of flesh. The first cut in a death of a thousand cuts.

When I woke the bed was empty. I had fallen onto the blue carpet where I lay dazed from clenching my eyes.

The phone was ringing.

'Hello.' The aroma of disinfectant was drifting out from the bathroom.

There was a silence, a scratching sound, the dial tone.

Jack wasn't in the room or bathroom. A feeling like death filled my stomach. I checked my stigmata then perched on top of the covers, flicked the TV on, kept the sound down, stared at a pop programme. Pop stars embarrass me, even the word. This Australian singer's face was like a lizard's. You could bash him over the head and make a pair of shoes out of him. How could anyone be a *pop star*? How can anyone be anything.

But you are dignified, eternal Adolf. The biggest star of the twentieth century. You impressed your enemies to death. We'll never forget you.

Really I don't want to sleep. Maybe I'll dream again? It's impossible to dream your own end. That's death.

You are immortal. The Adolf icon is ingrained in the soul of the world.

Has Jack paid our bill? Hotel rooms are all the same whatever the price, nonsense.

Rooms from the same price range are the same room maybe in a different colour with a different guest. Is there a deadline on our bill?

A room is a room. I'm on an island where the fat die young and there's a death sentence for betrayal.

There are shared rooms and single rooms, or single people alone in twin rooms. Why do things get spoiled?

I was starving, tempted to be wicked and search for some of Jack's jelly babies then eat them in bed without re-cleaning my teeth.

But at this moment, whether I think or not, fall asleep or stay awake, my long fringe is growing longer. Soon the stigmata will be completely covered. No one will ever know about them.

My eyes are blue again. Blue*ish*. Midnight blue in the dark. My stigmata are a sign the saints love me.

You are protecting me, beloved Adolf, twin soul, we share a birthday and a dream.

Next morning, staring across at the Palace Parlour waiting for the hunchback's celibate sister to bring me lukewarm orange juice and hard black toast (like the toast of my fantasies), I saw the man from the next room's back reflected in the electrified window beside me in my funereal silk dress. He's hunched into his gilt chair eating a fried egg, scouring the *Daily Stab*. Fried eggs fascinate me. How can anyone swallow them?

Outside the rain-drenched streets were dead.

Polish Mary plonked my juice down on the table and said, 'The rain might stop this afternoon.'

This rain will never stop. It will rain and rain forcing gut-buckets to stay indoors where they belong. Gut-buckets need shopping and eating to keep them going but this city closes when it rains. It's not versatile to catastrophe. Millions die in disasters. Everyone in London is insane.

She leaned against my table waiting for a response to her pronouncement. I sipped orange juice, watching the rind float on top. My lips made bloodstains on the rim of the glass.

When our neighbour from room 99 left the dining-room I nabbed his copy of the morning news. The slasher's made the cover again. BLOODTHIRSTY BEAST ALMOST CAUGHT. There's a call from the Fat Women of London to hang him.

The brave Asian wife and mother he ripped last night is half-dead but clinging to life in a secure hospital waiting to identify the sick fiend.

The Police found the bloodthirsty beast's weapon embedded in the maternal Stani's gut. Ethnic minority blood donors are asked to step forward.

I picked at the toast staring out the window pleased with what StarStab said about us today until the Pole started clearing up round me.

In the elevator my nipples were visible through the flimsy silk dress. No SS chic vest to keep me warm today. Suffering an aesthetic chill to look beautiful on his first sight of me this morning. Too bad he didn't come to breakfast.

At our room window I stood sniffing the blue flowers in a crystal glass on the ledge, watching the rain washing the street.

When the synagogue clock chimed I saw the fat man from yesterday sidle up in his long black car. It must be the same man. No one else could be that fat. He's wearing a huge pin-striped Savile Row suit with enormous shoes and a gangster black felt hat.

He disappeared into the massage parlour without looking up.

Those flowers smell peculiar. I sprayed Blue Dew from my atomiser into the air and sniffed again, shook back my hair, sprayed the stigmata. The unmistakable scent of the graveyard was still there.

'Never try to cover one smell with another,' Old Gorm used to mutter when Donald and I were chewing spearmint gum after slugging whisky.

A small ant, one that had lost the pack, meandered along my window ledge. It was dark brown and hungry.

Jack says ants send an advance party ahead of the main battalion to search for safe food. If they don't come back alive another party dances forward to do a recce. He showed me the dance they perform on the return journey if they liked the food, and the slouching step that's used if the scoff's made them sick. But if the second section goes missing in action the battalion moves next door.

I waited until my ant was in the middle of the ledge then squashed it under my boot. My sole left a faint imprint on the pale blue paint but there was no trace of the ant's corpse. Its body had been blitzed like Warsaw.

There was no sign of anyone in the street. The fat man's car had driven away without me noticing. The Stani shop was open but no one was going in.

I rushed out on the pretext of buying lemonade but forgot once outside and wandered over to Bishop Place. Balancing on the slippery wall, set to climb the broken railing, I saw three policemen cordoning off the chapel with white tape. I jumped down and hurried back to our room.

He'll be there already, I know it.

I bought a bar of cheap black chocolate from the Stani's (they were cleaned out of babies), asked Hose for my key – he didn't have it! – and rushed the stairs two at a time, huffing and puffing, damn near dead when I reached our door and knocked six times. No answer. He sleeps with the key in the lock so that no one can tiptoe in and surprise him.

Six more knocks (our code). No reply. 'Jack,' I whispered into the keyhole. Maybe he's pretending not to hear?

Knock. Knock. Knock. Knock. Knock. Knock.

The key was in my boot. That's why the banana didn't have it. He's told me before about not handing it in.

When you unlock a locked door jump in quick because there could be someone behind you poised to pounce.

The curtains were still open the way I left them.

He couldn't possibly be in the bathroom.

There was nothing under his bed. He takes everything out with him. He carries his life on his back.

Male footsteps in the corridor stopped outside our door. I touched my neck. The key turned in the lock. My rosary's gone. He's coming to get me.

Real assassins don't trust flickies. They can stick at the crucial thrust.

The door creaked open. The scream forming in my throat was silent. I imagined hurling myself off the balcony, prompting death by my own hand, resisting his will.

*

Chrissie, the bald maid, stuck her neck round the door giving me an appalling smile.

'I'm disturbing you,' she said, backing out.

I sank to the floor, grazing the stigmata with my fingernail. Definitely bigger.

Under my bed I could see a pile of notes. Fifties, tens. I lay on my back determined not to count them.

Another fucking Tuesday, I'm lying in my single bed
in the basement, arms folded across my chest, thinking about the last Empress of Austria. She never
looked a day older than thirty. I'm sixteen, I feel one
hundred and twenty-four, I'm not sure what age I
look in the light from behind the sky filtering through
the slats of my blue plastic blinds from Taiwan. At
least I'm seeing StarStab tomorrow.

'This is a cosy little room down here,' P. D. Hose
said as he showed me into this basement cupboard
with the single bed and white plastic mirror and lines
of ants trotting across the window ledge. 'Cheaper
than upstairs.' He slammed his hand down, blitzing
a battalion of ants. 'I live right next door.'

So I'm in the staff barracks of the Royal Hotel,
monitoring my stigmata, spinning out the money
Jack left, fretting about the fate of my flick-razor;
sharing this bunker with P.D., and the dwarf, and
Chrissie the maid who cries after midnight when she
can't forget the indignities of earning her crust from
scouring toilets.

I haven't washed yet today! I intend to take a
shower. The worst thing about leaving my room is

being recognised in the hallway. Having to say, 'Hello.' Being talked about afterwards. The idea of people knowing me is revolting. They know my real name here.

Then standing in the shower in my shoes trying not to breathe in or touch the edges, having to worry about how incurable diseases might be passed, always tortured by the choice of which member of staff was in here last. Sometimes I wash in the middle of the night when there's no chocolate in my room because water stops hunger. It sprinkles my longings away so that even if I had money I wouldn't eat.

I jumped out of bed feeling like death and went to the window. It's safe to open the blind. No one looks down. There are always overweight calves moving past, the undersides of carrier bags and briefcases, pudgy hands holding, trouser legs flapping above hairy ankles, women's feet in shoes that need heeled. It's remarkable the number of worn mud-encrusted spikes you see when it's not even raining. Those people must put their shoes away dirty. And most of the guilty ones are wealthy, thin and white!

An Arab businessman came out of the Palace Parlour ahead of a minor Lord. The lower ends of their bodies were distorted by the weight of their bulging cases.

The synagogue bells clang clang clanged twelve times. Those bells bang bang bang on and on all day long. At least there's not a rich Jewish wedding crowding everyone else off the pavement this morning, forcing us to listen to demented trivia.

I blooded my lips then lay back down on my bed leaving the blind up. The pale sky forced me to cover my eyes. In the shade every footstep sounds like his. But what if he comes for me and doesn't know where I am? I could will him to find me.

The slasher's silent. No frenzied assaults from the disturbed soul this month. He's off the front page. The headlines are yours again, beloved Adolf. They want the movie of your life banned before it's made – because of your power. It's beyond funny. Even the most immaculate triumph of the most brutal will couldn't have enabled one man to achieve what they credit you with. I should go and buy a newspaper. I have to take a shower before being seen in the street. Something terrible could happen in the shower, but dirty people are the end.

I noticed an ant on the window-ledge. It crawled under a book. I didn't recognise the cover. I can't remember reading a book in this room. What's it doing up there? That ledge is supposed to be kept clear. I tiptoed over to the window. The ant was hiding. The book's about God. My Sellotape was almost done. Sellotape makes a clean kill and the corpses are stuck there as a warning. There's millions of them covering this ledge. I dug my nails into the tape ripping a bit off then rattled the bible. The ant fell out, I smothered it.

It's Chrissie's day off. I can hear her television. There isn't a TV supplied with my room. If I had a TV I could watch black and white forties thrillers set in East Berlin, with glamorous actors with haircuts and profiles who're all dead now.

I cracked open a can of lemonade. When I lifted the glass to my lips I saw my face in it. Crystal and varnished oil paint and the doors of polished Mercedes convertibles are more seductive than real mirrors. I shouldn't be drinking lemonade. It's bound to be bad for my stigmata.

The synagogue clock clanged. I checked it against Napoleon's watch. Time for another cleansing.

Outside the shower room I stopped and listened.

The dwarf never locks himself in. P.D. doesn't wash. Chrissie hangs her wig on a hook while she sanitises herself after work. She came out without it on one day last week and had to dash back in. I saw her through the crack in my wall.

Definitely no running water in there today. I kicked the door open and leaped in.

'What's up? What do you want in here?' P.D. demanded.

He was standing under the dry hose wearing his hotel manager's outfit. Now I know why there are always large black footprints on the shower basin. He looked at my feet in disgust.

'Sorry,' I muttered. 'I didn't know there was anyone in here.'

'Don't worry. You're not disturbing *me*.'

I backed out the door. He put his hand on my left shoulder. I automatically reached for my razor, tricked again.

'Do you have a *boyfriend*?' he asked.

What can I say! I've already insisted Jack's coming back. In this situation I should definitely pretend to have a boyfriend. But the word embarrasses me. What if he's not a boy? Though saying *manfriend* would be just as bad. How do you know he's a man? And would it be insulting to call him a boy? Is the slasher a man or a boy?

'Well?' Hosie asked, poking his neck forward. People with bad posture are an eyesore. He bared his teeth. 'Do you or don't you?'

'Hmm . . .' I muttered, beaming blue fizz at him.

I returned to my room determined to leave it again today soon for an evening paper. There may be some news.

At five o'clock I crossed the street and fetched a *Daily Stab* (with the usual picture of you on the front), a new roll of Sellotape and some cheap chocolate. The wee Stani was wearing his tight tan leather mail-order suit with big smelly sneakers and off-white socks. He's like a melting jobbie on legs. When he smiled at me I looked the other way. How many women are forced to do that in these Eight 'til Lates?

'You'll get fat on that stuff,' he said, eyeing my three chocolate hearts as I left the shop. I slammed the door and ran across the road through the traffic and in the side entrance then down the staircase to my room.

Stuffing yourself stupid with chocolate will never

make you fat if you don't have a fat brain. You're definitely better off dead than fat. Fatties with no money are a waste of rations.

I dropped the *Stab* on the floor, placed the Sellotape on the ledge and lay on the thin blue carpet stretching my spine, listening to *Gotterdämmerung*, watching legs pass by above. A boy with boots like Jack's went by yesterday.

Time passes. Press the stigmata with my fingertips. Even mushier than it was this morning. I resprayed the marks of God with Blue Dew.

Everything bores me. Everything thrills me.

I turned my tape over and pulled the paper onto the floor beside me. Heil Heil Heil. Every day this newspaper is crammed full of fascinating facts.

The Jewish-American director has offered an unknown Aryan actor a fortune to impersonate you, beloved Adolf. They're filming in England, it's cheaper.

Beside your blazing image there's a small pic of someone I recognise but don't know. A man with plenty of chins and very little hair on his head. With a hat on and a big black car by his side he could be that fat guy I saw Jack talking to across the street. His name's Count Francis Louis Saadi, known as Fat Frank or Boy Lou, a rich Jew with a perfume business investing in a fascist movie! Heil Heil Heil.

The demos are still going strong. Pink lefties believe in free speech and free protest but only for themselves. They envy you. Your rallies were larger.

You needed an audience to live. You forced your dreams to come true. No one has the courage to replace you. Every bastard who tries can't bring himself to go far enough.

I scoured the whole paper twice but couldn't see a thing about the slasher. And StarStab hasn't a good word to say about our sign today. Maybe I shouldn't go to see her tomorrow?

But after all our meeting could change my life. That would be worth spending my last fifty.

On the other hand, the only thing worth believing in is your own will. Use your will to capture a fat man.

A rich fat man could keep me safe and protected somewhere where I wouldn't ever have to eat cheap chocolate again.

I went to the window. No obese soliciting bastards out there tonight. It's getting dark. I folded today's *Daily Stab* and placed it in my bin then lay down on the bed, but didn't go under the covers.

Sneaking looks at my face in the mirror I dreamed a new life in a Bavarian Schloss. A fortress surrounded by a shark-infested moat with an east and west wing and a guard-dog to sleep by my bed just in case. If you imagine something often enough it happens.

Will it to happen. Do something fucking fast with my fucking face. It's a crime not to.

Pick a card. Check Napoleon's watch before turning it over. Look at the card. The Sun. Excellent! The best card in the tarot. I have to act quickly. Before I lose my looks, my nerve.

Napoleon told us, 'Die before you give in.'

I moved from my bed to the floor and started doing sit-ups. I lost count.

There are things I would hate to die of: rabies, obesity, childbirth!

There are clean deaths like being shot to death staring at the firing squad after Last Rites from a Bishop in purple robes. Or gung-ho gutso deaths like being obliterated by dynamite or falling headfirst over a killer waterfall or smothering in the Sahara. There's another kind of death: things that sound good afterwards but aren't much fun at the time. Like being savaged by a wild beast or ravished by the slasher's blade.

And there are dirty deaths.

Death used to seem final but now picturing my body after the event has ruined the fantasy. People could come and look at me! It would spoil the thrill to die in this room.

Old Gorm used to say, 'There's worse things than dying . . .

Dying here would be a dirty death.

The Haugh is the only place I'd consider dying.

I rescued my *Stab* from the bin and tore out the picture of that fat man with the perfume business. The rip made a slash across his face. I'll sit at the window all day if necessary until he comes back. Then follow him.

I'll attack him with my will, force him to come here, put my whole spirit into it. Anything's possible if you keep a thin white decisive soul.

Triumph before it's too late. Before the money Jack left dwindles away. Before that stigmata takes over my life. Before I'm fucking seventeen years old.

Every time someone knocks on the door I think it's him. I adore sleep but can't. Tap tap tap. I knew it wasn't him, he wouldn't knock. Fresh blood on my lips. Open the door.

'Can I borrow your comb?' Chrissie the maid asked. She has a way of looking at me.

'I don't have a comb.' Maybe she can spot early signs?

'Just for five mins,' she said pleadingly, the soiled hands held in prayer. 'I dropped mine down the toilet.'

'I'd love to lend you my comb . . .' I started closing my door.

She smiled her appalling smile and said, 'I'm desperate.'

'. . . but I don't have one.'

I shut the door in her face. She's a waste of rations. I'm a determined thin white girl alone in a basement without my rosary.

*

The next day I woke up passionately wanting to be Chinese and always to wear midnight blue.

Hurrying out to my appointment I bumped into P. D. Hose in the corridor. He exposed his tongue and reminded me to hand in my key.

I walked outside thinking: I haven't enough money left to pay my bill. It was just a thought.

My appointment with StarStab was at eleven-fifteen so I risked a mini-cab outside the hotel, but it crashed in Piccadilly at eleven-five – leaving me ten minutes to run to Soho. StarStab's assistant, Lucky, had squeezed me in on a last minute cancellation. There wasn't likely to be another opportunity like this for decades. StarStab didn't *have* to see me, I'm not even a regular. And now this cab had smashed into the back of a nigger brown Volkswagen. No one was killed.

A split second before impact I raised my knees and lowered my chin and held my head between my arms the way Jack showed me in an elevator that had lost its brakes. The top of my skull was momentarily hurled into the back of the driver's seat. He was an ethnic, with skin that familiar shade of melted shit, evidently without a first language because he sprang out of his cab and swore at the other driver in English.

I stumbled out of the car and ran along Piccadilly. Every time I looked back there was a man behind me. By the time I reached StarStab's cellar there was sweat on my upper lip, humiliating.

I clanged the broken crucifix knocker six times.

Lucky stuck his head round the door and muttered, 'You're twenty minutes late.' One of his ears was missing.

Fifteen, by Napoleon's watch, but I nodded agreement, adding apologetically, 'I had to walk. My taxi crashed.'

He didn't believe me. 'Wait here,' he said. 'I'll see if she can fit you in.'

Ten minutes later Lucky ushered me into a red cubicle, demanded fifty notes, and told me to remove my clothing. I was still dressed when he came back with a white gown.

'Hurry up,' he said. 'We have someone else coming at twelve.'

He stood looking the other way waiting for me to change then ushered me into a round room without windows. The whirl of a second-hand washing machine was audible in the distance.

'Your fortune's your own business, reveal it to no one,' he said before disappearing.

StarStab joined me at the unbalanced table. There was a metal cross pinned to her left breast. It was making a hole in the sleeveless embroidered tunic she was wearing. Her outfit showed off the flaps of flab hanging from her upper arms. Without saying a word she inclined her head towards her crystal ball, unexpectedly looking up imploringly at me with the eyes of a guilty saint.

Four minutes? Five? How much longer could we wait for inspiration.

Eventually she lit a cigarette and started doling out the tarot.

'Pick seven cards.' Before I was finished she said:

'*Avoid* travelling on trains.

'You will be found by unexpected *riches*.

'There's a man with a *black* soul watching over you.'

That made me sit up. She upturned my cards without letting me see. I know what that means. I've picked Death as well as La Maison de Dieu.

StarStab's bloodshot eyes reflected my apprehensive blue gaze. She stroked my upturned palm with clammy fingers, saying dramatically, 'Your destiny comes first. Remember that.' She paused. And then: 'You are running . . . I smell Death . . .' She gagged on her own smoke. 'What is that smell?! I demand to know? What is it?'

'Blue Dew?'

'Be quiet,' she hissed, fleetingly opening her eyes, grabbing the crystal to her breast.

'You are running,' she continued passionately, 'running towards the great dictator, the most famous man in the world. Or are you running away from him?' She flung the crystal from her, aggressively demanding a reaction. 'Help me! Help me!'

'Is he fat?'

She grabbed both my hands.

'Are you running away?'

Her eyes were desperate. All I could feel was my own soul racing, the way it does in sleep, falling uncontrollably towards its fate.

Her body slumped closer. Her cigarette had

extinguished itself. She was about to tell me. She really does know and she was about to say it without understanding when Lucky rapped on the door.

Her grip relaxed. Her breathing calmed down.

'Next month,' she said reassuringly, 'you come and see me again.'

Lucky led me into the changing room, waited, then unbolted the main exit for me.

As I was climbing the crumbling stairwell, a tear on my cheek, he said unexpectedly, 'A broken heart is always cured within seven weeks.'

I would have said ten, or twenty, in case seven had already passed. A lifetime to be on the safe side.

There wasn't a fucking taxi in sight. Just as I went down the steps into the subway an overweight woman with dry dyed hair and blood-contused dents below each eye thrust up the wrong side of the stairway and crashed into me.

I landed flat on my back with a view of her flabby gooseflesh legs and the congealed scab on her ankle next to the coloured strap of her working-class heels. She wobbled then keeled over on top of me.

She has one of those growths on her neck that I've noticed before attached to poor whites. A blob of flesh too big to be an ordinary mole, clinging to her throat, mottled like the skin of a rotting corpse. Cancerous? Contagious?!

A man pulled her off and asked if I was all right but I just stood up and ran for it. Round the corner out of sight I kept walking fast, watching my back, determined never to take the train again. StarStab's right: who wants to be squashed up against endless collections of fat knackered useless eaters of indeterminate colour and stink. Lank hair, round shoulders, squashed faces, necks poked forward. Where are they all going? I'd rather die than take a train again. Rich fat men don't need trains. Being rich and fat goes hand in hand. The fat die conveniently young.

I went into The Eagle and was comforted by symmetrical lines of red leather chairs with black backs. I sat in the window seat and ordered hot chocolate. It cost a gold coin and roasted my tongue.

While I was sitting there I didn't think about Jack at all. He's not on my mind these days. There's only room for my mission to capture that fat man.

Before I had finished swallowing my drink someone I recognised came in but I managed to leave without being seen.

The fat man's long black car stops across the street every other day at three minutes past twelve by Napoleon's watch. He drives himself. The big wheels of his enormous car trample the road like a tank. A family of nine could live inside it with their pet wolf.

He steps with his shiny decisive size thirteen feet across the pavement and disappears into the Palace Parlour for eleven minutes.

He is of course Count Francis Louis Saadi of *Daily Stab* fame, the ugliest man in the world. Uglier than all my mother's ex-boyfriends put together. Almost as ugly as Uncle Ned (who doesn't count as a man).

This fat billionaire's old but not too old. It's impossible to tell exactly what age from my basement window because successful men like that all look the same age when sometimes they're not in real life. They share the same hairstyle (bald with curly bits) and clutch the same dream. They need attention to make them real.

I started waking early to see his pin-striped Savile Row legs disappear through the doorway. If I step on the blue stool and strain my neck back I catch sight of his hat when he comes out. He wears it low concealing his passionate flabby cheeks.

Last Thursday a derelict asked him something but the Count didn't betray curiosity. He's not spoken to anyone else in the street since I saw him ages ago with Jack.

There's no difficulty waking up to spy on him because the synagogue bells clang twelves times at noon. I'm able to position myself in the Stani's doorway ready for Fat's arrival. Close-up this fat rich old man in his loose-fitting designer gangster suit is obviously foreign. His skin is dark, but not too dark. He's dark*ish*. In lamplight he'd just look like a white man with a tan. He could be an Arab, he could be a Jew, but he definitely isn't a jungle bunny. He's like an ugly movie star you can't keep your eyes off.

Because of my new strengthened will I start jumping out of bed even earlier. Looking forward to it the night before, becoming more and more animated, deciding in advance how tight my skirt should be, washing my hair in the morning in thrilling cold water and wearing heels and scarlet lips, making sure I'm walking past his car just as he emerges with his big grin.

Coincidences like my presence in the doorway of the Stani newsagent's, or the sight of me strolling past his parked car at exactly the same time every second day are not suspicious to fat men. Regularly at that hour I could be going to work or exercising my dog. Or I could be going to fetch my essentially huge immaculately groomed ferocious but loyal German Shepherd to take it for a walk.

'Good morning.' That was the first thing the Count said to me in my whole life. I smiled but kept going, his smell up my nostrils, the unwashed eyes following me.

Two days later he added, 'How nice to see you. How are you?' in a convincing pre-war Warsaw accent.

At our next meeting I said Hello to him. That was quite a success. He asked my name.

'So-phi-ra,' he repeated. 'I like that name.' My face reflected in his windscreen looked the way it does when I'm nervous but pretending.

We fell silent. My eyes strayed to the Palace Parlour's window sign: *Lovely Dining Companions for Discreet Gentlemen.* Inevitably I wondered if he lunches with the same gorgeous creature every time.

Count Saadi's big face turned scarlet.

He said, 'One of my propert-ees is upstairs . . . So-phi-ra.'

Every second day for two weeks we met on the pavement between the Parlour and his car. We smiled at each other in the rain, or the weak morning sunlight, or under insecure clouds. He would say my name, 'So-phi-ra,' though I never uttered his name out loud.

When we met he told me a little about himself; or asked me something. It was standing on the pavement beside his big car that I found out more about his perfume business. The Count wholeheartedly believes in enhancing natural body odours. His perfumes don't mask a person's smell, they *encourage* it. His Contessa company manufactures a range of sniffs for specific sensations: how you are after an energetic kiss, a glowing walk in the park, a midnight phone call with the object of your desires. His personalised body odour range makes him a packet.

Leaning in close he told me, 'So-phi-ra, you have a love-lee smell . . .' And I don't wear perfume!

We didn't discuss Jack. Fat men can't stand rivals. They may not even know each other. That conversation I witnessed from our first-floor room window could have been innocent.

When we'd been meeting regularly for three weeks the Count offered to drive me home. But I said, 'No, it isn't far, I can walk.' My lips were red and determined.

He sat in his car and watched me cross the street then disappear in the side entrance of the Royal. Once safely out of sight I ran downstairs two at a time and checked my face in the plastic mirror on my room wall to make sure the stigmata had been covered while I was talking to him, then hurried to the window to see if his gleaming car was still jammed between other cars up there in the street.

Each time after checking I sank back in relief onto my bed. Until the day I stood breathless on the stool straining to see and his big black car had already turned into Oxford Street out of sight.

After that omen we didn't meet again for ten days. He didn't turn up. He was in Tripoli. For all I know he went there to have lunch with another lovely companion.

But soon after that separation he begged me to share his enormous flat in the top floor of a building overlooking Park Lane.

'So-phi-ra,' he pleaded. 'Don't leave me there all alone. Anything but that!' He stroked my naked fingers. 'I can't bear it a day more!'

Part Two

Case White

'Purity is absolutely invulnerable as purity . . .
no violence can make it less pure.'

SIMONE WEIL

The day Count Saadi changed my life I waited for
him in reception watching my aqua eyes in the mirror
behind the desk, my small black bag between my feet
on the royal-blue carpet. Cussons was making up
my bill.

As the synagogue clock struck noon P. D. Hose
bananaed over to me and said sternly, 'You won't
get a better room anywhere in London.'

I bared my teeth.

'Suit yourself,' P.D. said to my back.

The Count appeared in the doorway. As he walked
towards me a monstrous trail of his own perfume
settled on the carpet.

'Ah, So-phi-ra,' he said. 'At last!'

Handing my bill to the Count, Cussons had a bewildered look on his face, like a newsreader determined not to laugh. He doesn't want to smirk because it's a solemn subject he's paid to take seriously, but his face betrays him. It's twitching. Nerves? Uneasiness on my behalf? Sadism.

The Count paid cash, said my name again, touched my hair, picked up my bag, and we ran down the portico steps together crossing the damp pavement to his big car. Most people didn't look at us funny because a lot of breathless overweight men hang around with thin white girls. It's the sort of thing you only notice once you've done it yourself. Like buying a blue car then realising *everyone* has one.

He'd left his engine running. Waiting upstairs had been good fate.

Inside the car we didn't speak. He broke the silence once by saying, 'So-phi-ra,' then blushing. He might have blushed, with skin like that it's hard to tell. And close-up in daylight I can't bring myself to look. I examine him in the dark or when he isn't likely to catch me.

At his building in Park Lane the doorman, who's slouching through a losing battle with bad breath, took the car keys. My fat man said to this hunched working-class animal, 'This is Miss Sophira. Admit her always.' The specimen looked at me through half-closed eyes then turned away.

All the way up to the top floor in the smoked-glass lift Count Saadi held my hand. In the mirrored wall I stared at myself shaking my fringe forward. The Count kept looking at his watch. I could see him out the corner of my eye.

Straight away he showed me my celestial blue room at the end of the marble hallway. We stood in the doorway staring at the big glossy bed smothered with pillows and the furniture satin-smooth like the skin of a painted Madonna.

Huge jugs of frightening pale flowers cluttered the cold floor. The high bare window was open admitting a breeze that was almost reflected in the baroque ballerina mirror filling the opposite wall. Immediately I knew I would wear white in this room.

When he came towards me I looked away.

Another thrilling Tuesday morning in January, the Count's just left, I'm scrubbing my teeth again in the gold-plated marble bathroom which joins my room to his. His perfume hasn't completely drowned out the other smell. When I was young I hated using our toi after Mother for that reason. The only bathroom I've ever really loved is the upstairs one at The Haugh.

At sunrise the fat man climbs out of his bed and comes into this bathroom. He sits on the gold toi for a good long time, calling out to me, 'So-phi-ra, are you asleep?' puffing his own brand of perfume from the atomiser kept on the cistern. Then he thuds into my room for his morning kiss. I don't have to. He has his pride. No one's being forced. But he likes this one thing every morning before disappearing to his office.

My eyes are closed until he reaches the bed. When the footsteps stop I part my lips and refuse to think.

But this morning I could hardly get my mouth open. He had to force his tongue between my teeth. My jaw froze. I trained my eyes on his marked neck willing the ritual to end. But when the sucking was almost over I jerked my teeth together and bit his puffy gum!

He didn't say anything but his face fell. Of course close-up he's exceptionally fat. The flesh of his cheeks trembles in rhythm to his husky breathing.

'So-phi-ra,' he said. 'How are you? Have a nice day.'

I don't mind him saying things like that because he isn't the sort of fat guy to demand an answer to a daft question.

As soon as I heard the front door slam shut I ran into our bathroom and started scrubbing my teeth in fizzy mineral water, checking my stigmata in the mirrored walls as I spat up toothpaste froth.

The mark of God's an angrier ruby red but the growth could be at a standstill. Now that my hair covers it effortlessly it's not spreading so fast. And the Count has given me a Chinese silk veil, his first gift, because we're stigmata twins: his neck is disfigured with a concentration camp chic tattoo almost covered by the fuzzy black hairs which grow all over his body. He was a twin star who escaped the scientific research chamber. And every year at this time the Count's thin brother Robert leaves him at home while he travels to the Holy Land to thank God formally for saving them and making them rich and providing them with more than enough to eat.

When I finished cleaning my teeth I went from the bathroom into his room, sliding across the gleaming gold floors naked, because once the Count's gone to his office he doesn't come back until evening scoff time.

I bounced on his obscenely large bed, big enough for a giant widthways and lengthways. In this bed he can roll for miles before falling off the edge.

But it's easy living with this fat man. I like him. His fat's his only indulgence. But he constantly questions me about my diet when we're seated together in the small sitting-room at night with the fluted silk carmine lamps lit and the fire glowing, the low table perched between us covered with cartons of take-away food, the luxuriously gloomy lighting duplicating the room through the high bare windows.

'So-phi-ra, what did you eat today?' He leans forward staring at my face, his thin livid lips set.

I've tried but I can't eat. He knows I'm lying when I describe the black toast and lemon scrambled eggs I swallowed with raspberry juice at brekkers. The animated white yoghurt and bright yellow bananas and feverishly pink strawberries for lunch. The high-energy nut snacks. The tall glasses of carrot juice.

He slouches in his chair staring at me, his small charcoal eyes submerged in flesh, and says, 'You'd better eat something, you have to eat.'

The Count eats. He shits constantly but never loses weight. When he's not in his office he's in our toilet.

But it's definitely acceptable living with this fake Jewish Count who's pretending to be an Arab. He's the fattest guy I've ever hung around with but it doesn't bother him. Though he uses indescribable words. Once he called me something that I could never repeat to anyone ever. I couldn't even say it out loud if I was locked in a room by myself. I hope I never hear that word again as long as I live.

He's the ugliest man I've ever spoken to in London but he has great arms. The best arms I've ever seen, and the best Warsaw accent you ever heard, and a nose and mouth and two sallow ears. He even drinks whisky and smokes cigars, sucking and wheezing, creating new brown stains on his teeth, increasing his breathlessness and blood pressure. We have an excellent doctor, a redhead called Humphrey, who has a blonde receptionist with better teeth than me! She checks the Count's blood every week. Humphrey provides pills to control diarrhoea.

Every time Count Saadi does a jobbie he covers his big bottom in cologne after spraying the bathroom for my benefit with an appropriate scent from his personalised body odour range. But his twin brother's returning from his annual pilgrimage soon.

Before lunging for the toilet to sick up his Indian dinner last night he said, 'Robert's coming back ver-ee quick,' an uncertain cheeser sprawling across the plump crimson cheeks.

When he had finished being sick he waddled back into the dusky little room, sprawled his body across the blue satin sofa and said, 'My brother's an excel-lent cook.'

He smiled again. Smiling suits him. His grin spreads across the substantial cheeks with comforting regularity. I'm glad, because I like things to stay the same. I don't like surprises, especially surprises involving other people.

There's a locked door in Fat's bedroom which leads to his brother's bedroom, the only locked room in the Count's vast high-in-the-sky flat. A lukewarm tropical smell oozes through the keyhole. There are mirrors and plants and framed photographs in there.

His brother's kitchen has millions of utensils sharpened and ready on the wooden walls. His refrigerator is huge. His oven even bigger. There's a scrubbed table littered with chopping boards in the lunatic centre of the dark room with the funereal blinds down. The kitchen is the only room with blinds. We never go in there.

Once or twice since moving in last month I've stood on the threshold wondering if I should hunt for ice-cream in the freezer.

I slid along the marble hallway with the window at the end overlooking Park Lane, turned into our little room with the lamps, put *Wuthering Heights* in the VCR, shut the sound off, practised Basai Dai listening to Wagner. The silver light dazzling in the bare windows converted the holy red room to an open effervescent temple close to Heaven, but the feeling of being watched annoyed me.

Turning *Parsifal* up full blast I slid to the bathroom and ran the taps having my soul uplifted above the din of crashing water. Heroic music heroic minds heroic men.

'You take too many baths,' the fat Count told me

soon after I moved in here. He never explained his remark. People are like that. They don't say why the bath isn't good for you they just make their complaint, standing watching you with protruding lower lip.

Relaxing my white body under the dazzling blue liquid, I ate two packs of Jack's favourite jelly babies, sprayed my face with water from a fizzy French spring, painted my blood lips then stood up, dripping myself dry, unpinning my new long hair, checking the stigmata, arranging my veil, choosing a dress from the crazy pile on my bedroom floor.

By the time the tape finished I was ready to take a taxi to Chinatown, becoming more and more excited now that I can afford silk lanterns, bubbles, slippers (for wee feet), pyjamas I'm small enough for, two fake Ming bracelets – one for each white wrist – a hand-painted screen without a price, a giant's fan for when I lie in bed all day too hot, and my first Chinese dress.

A new dress will always make me want to go on living. The scarlet colour matches my lips but the Oriental saleswoman didn't believe it would fit me.

'You're not Chinese,' she said.

'I know,' I replied, holding my breath, studding myself in, ecstatic with the reflection in her paint-stained mirror. In any language there are two types of shop assistants. The superior kind with haircuts and overgrown melons and the round-shouldered hags with uncontrollably staring eyes and nervous breakdown mouths. They all fear me in the end. I'm good at kill or be killed situations.

I chose a pair of velvet jewel-encrusted slippers and hurried out, eager to try on my thrilling new dress alone while gazing into my ballerina mirror.

Waiting to hail a cab I became ravenous, thought about eating in The Eagle, instead bought a bag of small cute yellow cakes and a *Daily Stab*. There's been no news of the slasher for weeks. Everyone's forgotten about him. But he has one more victim to claim.

The yellow cakes tasted disgusting. When my cab stopped for a red light on Piccadilly I spat a mouthful out the window. A Colonel with whiskers driving a Mercedes winked at me. I wondered if maybe I should have ordered more made-to-measure satin underwear from the little old man in Soho who sews?

When I reached home the Count was there! It's beyond funny. He *never* shows up before dinnertime. But it's three-thirty by Napoleon's watch and he's splayed on our toi with the door open.

I knew he was in before I saw him. There's a different atmosphere in an occupied flat, even a huge one, and Fat has an aura as well as his unmistakable smell. His smell's in all the rooms, even the ones I've never seen him go into. When he's close it's overpowering.

'So-phi-ra!' he called.

Without a word I threw my thrills on my bed and tiptoed across the hall. After twenty-two minutes he still hadn't shown his face.

Even standing behind the bathroom door I couldn't hear a sound. When he's constipated he switches the taps on and off for something to do, or sings at the top of his voice in warning. And when it's the other thing that's keeping him in there he has to stand up and flush the toi a couple of times to clear space for his next splurge.

The door of his room was ajar. Pushing it with my toe I saw the Count kneeling on the tiles over a carton of custard flan, pushing it into his open jaws with his short fat fingers. Two utterly empty cartons were abandoned on the floor beside him. His face – in his mirror – was red and wobbly, his lips yellow at the edges.

Momentarily disturbed, his reflection looked up at me then continued until the third carton was licked clean. The Count raised himself from his knees and said, trembling, 'My brother's definitely coming back tomorrow.' He kicked the cardboard boxes under his bed and muttered like a prayer, 'He's an excellent cook.'

We both looked at a framed picture newly placed on his Arabic bedside table of a sour cadaverous Jewish man with a kosher wig plonked on his flat wide head.

He's insanely ugly. A thin version of the Count. An unidentical identical twin.

When he went back out my stomach sank, I realised I loved him and felt pathetic.

I couldn't wait for him to come back home! Eventually I crossed the road to the park and stood out of sight watching for his car. When it finally came down Park Lane and stopped outside our building I ran through the traffic and made it into the lift just before the doors closed.

'Ah, So-phi-ra,' he said. 'Such lovely lips, slender hips – where have you been? How are you?' He grinned, revealing his cinnamon teeth. My heart beat faster. He put his squat hairy hand on my arm. He never touches me in the elevator! I thought I was going to die. Maybe he suspects?

'I was at the park,' I said. He looked at me in disbelief. All the way up to the top floor he just stood staring at me, saying nothing. There was an odd expression on his flabby face.

That night I shook when he came near me, and couldn't talk in case my voice was stupid. When he enshrined himself in the toi I sneaked out and paced up and down Park Lane thinking, 'It's so degrading. How can I get out of this?'

Sick of being in love already and it had just started. Aware there's no solution. Even if I left that would guarantee nothing and I have stigmata and might have to start seeing National Health doctors.

Even if the fat one decided to love me eventually one of us would get fed-up or die.

Dying's fashionable. Jack isn't going to die. He hates copy-cats.

Dying could be a thrill, but not tonight.

When I arrived back, breathless, the Count was

sprawled in his crushed blood velvet chair smoking the biggest cigar you've ever seen. Only one of the lamps was glowing. This pink sunset reflected the room onto the night like a mirror.

'So-phi-ra,' he said, patting the cushion at his feet. 'Where have you been?'

I wanted to go sit by him so I said, 'Mind your own business Fattie,' and went to my room, slammed the door, and stood holding my breath, listening.

At eight-thirty Napoleon's watch stopped. I couldn't be bothered winding it up. Ages later I heard Fat's footsteps going down the hall, then the front door opened and closed.

After putting all the lamps out I sat on the sea-blue satin sofa, TV on, sound down. A re-run of a crime show. Vroom, vroom. In the window I saw me with my feet up, my white bright face, hair in my eyes, lipstick off a bit at the edges. The corners of the mouth are the first places to sag. Mother advised against chewing bubblegum and sucking XL penises and unnecessary smiling.

But I don't intend to have anything to do with imperfection. Neither did you, beloved one. Your passion for death was exaggerated because you couldn't live with impurity.

I hate him. Where is he? Why doesn't he come?

Anything could happen. It could just as easily be good. I could die and if not I can watch all-night TV. Eventually he'll come back.

I longed for the old carefree days when the Count

and I had flirted on the pavement and I hadn't known I loved him but just got on with it with Jack as my broken heart.

It started raining. I could hear it join the roof. *Newsnight* came on. I flicked the sound up and listened to the intro music. It's comforting, like hearing him come in: the elevator door closes, his key turns, his footsteps come down the hall . . .

The phone rang twice then stopped. My stomach muscles tightened. Flicking the TV off I jumped up, catching sight of my hair reflected in the shadowed window as the ringing started up again. When I picked it up I didn't say Hello. There was a sound like long fingernails scratching broken glass. The man making the noise was first to hang up.

I dropped the receiver and stared at my hair in the window. Long hair leads to fear of loss. Eventually it destroys you.

Outside across the road a thin megalomaniac in a dial-a-disguise kit was staring across at our building, the collar of his military leather trencher turned up against the wind. He looks like you.

It's pitch black in here. It must be impossible to see in an unlit window up this high.

Maybe he has infra-red night sights?

When I heard the Count's key in the lock I tiptoed across to my room and lay pretending to be asleep.

His big black feet stopped outside my door. Everything was still for a long time then he went into his bedroom.

The footsteps crossed the marble floor to our bathroom. He ran the taps first then sat on the gold toi. I heard him standing up to open the skylight. If I'm ever bored in there I stare at the stained glass Virgin painted onto the roof window.

Fat started whistling. To be sure of the tune I climbed out of bed and listened through the wall. The song sent my heart Whoosh!

When the gold toi thundered its flush I ran back to my luminous white bed, soul pounding through my flesh, begging God to help me just this once for old times' sake.

But all the lights went out.

He didn't lie awake in the dark fretting. His snoring started almost immediately. If my watch was wound I could have told you exactly how long it took the fat bastard to fall into Nod.

All night I thought about confessing, killing him, crying. The morphine from tears makes it all better but I couldn't cry. What's the point? Feeling better is temporary. You may as well conquer the worst. Just get it over with. Get a new fat man? One you couldn't possibly love. Fattish baldish men are all the same. Pick an even richer one you wouldn't be addicted to in a million years because of some irreversible fault he can never change.

Passion addiction. Always on the verge of degradation. It won't happen again.

Why did I decide to love this fat man? Maybe I'm trying to act perverse to shock myself? He isn't that ugly. Some days quite handsome, in a way. If I start daydreaming that I'll get a shock next time I force myself to look.

Mother used to say, 'If you want someone good-looking take a photograph.'

Maybe if he wanted a full rumpy-pumpy instead of a good-morning greeting and a live-in chaperone it would be easier to feel defiled?

Running away would be imperative.

I went into our bathroom and fed my sweaty mouth from the tap. My face was white and dead. When he comes for his killer kiss tomorrow morning I'll look like death.

There wasn't a sound from his room. Even the snoring had died.

Donald and I used to have little chats in the dark. Sometimes he shone his torch on my face to see what I was thinking. We always slept in the upper bunk, one at the top, one at the bottom. We insisted on wearing the same colour of pj's.

One night he asked me if I was going to die.

'Are you?'

'Dying's silly,' he said.

Just as I was falling asleep he whispered, 'We're twins. We'll die at exactly the same time.'

'What if it comes for me first?'

'I'll beam blue fizz at it.'

Outside the sky covering Park Lane was absolutely black. I lay back down on my bed with the stigmata veil covering my face. Confusion can't last forever. It can't kill me because a smart heart can't be broken twice, can it? Not on an island. Not by a man a million times uglier than me.

I can't sleep. Trying to sleep is trying to die. I'll never do it.

When the silk veil slipped off my face sunlight stabbed me awake. Outside big cars were thundering down Park Lane. I reached for my leather sunglasses.

He's gone. He left without taking his Goodbye kiss. He doesn't like me anymore. It's always the same when you fall in love.

I knew Fat had disappeared before seeing the alarming time on his clock because his aura wasn't in the flat.

But there's the comforting smell of his stale shit and effusive perfume in the bathroom. I climbed onto the edge of the tub, enjoying the cold marble on my bare feet, and pushed open the skylight.

When I lifted the toi lid a gust of wind splashed one of his things around. Only last week the sight of it would have made me sick.

I pulled the chain and sat down.

Just when the process was at the unstoppable stage the front door opened and heavy footsteps came down the hall. I concentrated hard in an insane effort to speed things up.

It might have been possible to stand and run and block the two doors, but something might drop from me onto the floor. Then it would have to be picked up!

Two big black feet came into my room. My heart thudded. My face burned under the glasses. Queasily I called out, 'Just a minute!'

When the thing plopped into the water a bony horrible man with emaciated cheeks appeared in my bathroom and said, 'Hi, I'm Bobbie – Lou's twin.' He smelled of cat and was wearing a clumsily knitted jungle-bunny brown cardigan. Nigger brown is a colour I grew up with. The Haugh is full of dark wood.

He held out his hand to shake. He'd make an excellent ugly woman. The sort the slasher would murder on sight, if he was still up to his tricks.

In the mirror he watched me enveloping myself in a giant white towel while he washed his hands slowly at my sink with my Vitamin E soap.

'I'm going to take a bath now,' I said, starting the violent rushing water, tossing in some Blue Dew.

'You know you've got a great face.'

Has he noticed my stigmata? I gave him a bad stare and said nothing. The sight of him was causing an ugliness attack. I didn't want to look, but you have to keep at least one eye on people like that. He might try to rape me. Jack could at least have left my razor.

He hugged his cardigan closer to his body and asked, 'Have you ever thought about using that amazing face of yours?' He grinned at me up close revealing false teeth bigger than Old Gorm's. The muscles by my mouth and eyes twitched. He sat down on the toilet lid.

'You know you'll be more comfortable if you sit too.'

'I'm going to take a bath.' I tested the water with my toes.

'It would be a crime if you didn't do something with that face.' As his jaws widened into an insane smile his cloying smell rushed full force out of the animated pores.

'What would you like for breakfast?'

'I never eat breakfast.' The look on his face reminded me of Gorm and the force-feeding times. She's an old woman who's always been an old man.

He slithered off to his kitchen swinging his evil hips. I tiptoed to my open door and listened.

He raised the blinds, lifted the big freezer lid, tutting away, slammed it down then came out into the hall. I jumped back, shutting my door and standing behind it holding it closed with my body.

He unlocked the door of his room and slid something across the floor.

My brain was busy with too many decisions. How could I enjoy a bath with him loitering? He could barge in any minute with the lunch menu.

His fusty stench was still in my room even though I sprayed Blue Dew violently in the air immediately above my Nefertiti nose.

I rammed a chair under the door knob then lay in

the deep blue water feverishly stuffing jelly babies into my mouth.

After a quick dip I dressed in Luftwaffe combat trousers and starched white Italian shirt and sat on my bed re-painting my toe-nails, wondering what to do, flicking through a magazine full of pictures of German men. He was still out there. Was he going to stay in *all day*?

I overheard him on the phone ordering yummies for our tummies.

If I go outside he'll definitely come in here.

It was four o'clock. The Count wouldn't be home for at least another three hours, maybe three and a half. He may not come in until midnight.

In the distance I could hear the twin beating hell out of a piece of dough or breaking a chicken's neck or something domestic in his kitchen.

Someone buzzed our doorbell six times. The Count's brother opened it.

'Thank you, thank you!' he called out, closing the door again quickly.

At five o'clock I gave myself a good talking to: What am I *doing*? Am I *afraid* of an ugly thin cook? Me?!

He was talking to someone on the kitchen phone. It sounded like another grocery order. The washing-machine was churning. When I went in and sat down, flicking through his copy of the *Stab*, I noticed with a jump that the kitchen window overlooks the eagle cemetery I followed Jack to that night. It seems like years ago. It's dead down there today.

'You haven't eaten your lunch.'

It's practically dinner time! He's beyond funny.

He snatched the inky paper out of my hand, smiling at the photograph of you on the front page, dropped it on the tiled counter, and plonked a bowl of thick red soup with stuff floating in it down in front of me.

Out of the corner of my eye I could see his huge knives and pitchforks and flat sharp spades hanging on the wooden wall. He stood with his back to me adding the final spices to a Jewish stew bubbling in a big pot on the stove. After that he rinsed a large chicken and laid it with its legs open ready to rip. He selected an enormous knife from the wall and stuck it into the chicken's crack, peeling the skin backwards. It came off in one. He slung the useless parts in the bin and started grating a hard pale yellow vegetable I couldn't identify. The awful sound imitated the noise sleazy pencils make when used blunt.

Through the washing-machine door I could see the Count's red and white striped bloomers swirling round and round. I couldn't bring myself to eat the soup so I crumbled a piece of bread into my fist and swallowed the dismembered bits.

Bobbie was studying me from behind a baking bowl of whipped chocolate double cream as if he didn't like my face as much in this light.

'You don't want your soup.' He snatched the bowl

away replacing it with a colourful salad ready-pre-pared from the fridge. 'I know *exactly* what Lou likes.'

Beaming blue fizz at him, I stabbed cucumber and tomatoes and lettuce with the small silver fork, listening for screams, and reached for the paper, pressing it breathing distance from my nose. StarStab said something unpleasant about us and there wasn't a thing on TV for me.

'Lou's favourite,' he said, looking not at me but at a whale of pink carbohydrate he was vigorously appliquéing with chocolate cream. It looked like a real cake, the sort of thing you might buy from an expensive shop. The sneak had obviously had it delivered and was now customising it to fool Fat into thinking he baked it for him!

While he was bent over the freezer I peeped at the surface. In bold tabloid CAPS it said IT'S GOOD TO BE BACK BRO. He had drawn two smiling moon faces, his and his, one on each side of the cake.

'How long have you lived in London?'

'Since the war.'

He smiled, bending over to stuff a crammed tray of raspberry turnovers into the red-hot oven.

'The Gulf?'

He held his palm to his forehead sending a stale whiff of his mouldy smell to contaminate my air space. 'The war! The war! The war that claimed our whole family. We were children . . . Left all alone together in that place . . .'

'The Russian Revolution?'

He ripped off his rubber gloves and sat down

opposite me at the table. One large hand rested between his legs, the other was concealed in the pocket of his nigger brown cardi. He leaned in close so that I could see my dreamy blue eyes reflected in his small peep-holes. He cleared his throat for a long story. As his thick voice droned I puffed my atomiser drenching the condensated air with Blue Dew.

The twins Ezra and Irv were brought up in a concentration camp. – One of those places on TV where everyone has short hair, wears baggy clothes, speaks lyrically and has a saintly regard for his fellow captive. Their souls are so pure it's surprising anyone minds dying.

But Ezra and Irv are clever children, they change their names to Bob and Lou, and escape before mad Doctor Riefenstahl converts them into lampshades.

The cook leans closer to me, laughing softly.

The young twins haven't learned to be passive yet, they don't believe in failure. They see the Sonderkommando are busy men, outnumbered, unable to guard all of the damned all of the time.

The twins slip into the forest and keep on running until they reach London and when the war is over they eat and eat and become big twins, and they slave and save money for food and a home and a new religion and more money to prevent anything bad happening ever again. Until the hour of their revenge when Bob's clever twin brother Lou finances a movie about you, beloved Adolf, the story of your successes.

That's the dignified way to win the peace: make a profit out of your worst enemy!

*And the twins are living happily ever after. They have
each other, they have always had each other, they will
always have each other, they need nothing else, they never
disagree and . . .*

The Count's key turned in the lock. Bobbie put his
finger to his lips, sucking in his breath. The Count
strolled into the kitchen in his subdued forties suit,
his eyes looking out from under the gunmetal-grey
Fedora.

'Ah, Robert,' he said, kissing his cheeks.

'Ah, Sophira.' He frowned as he kissed me. 'How
nice to see you. Both of you!'

He made a fuss about sniffing each dish, including
the skinless chicken abandoned bare on the counter.
He laughed appreciatively at the absurd cake, haul-
ing Bobbie's body in close to his for a congratulatory
hug. The spluttering sound embarrassed me.

'Robert, Sophira,' he said. 'Will you excuse me?'

He stuck his thumb into the chocolate cream,
sucked it clean, hesitated, then left the kitchen.

I stood up, grabbing the cook's copy of the *Stab*.
He almost whispered, 'You know it wasn't such a
bad idea?'

'Huh?' My hand was on the door. He covered my
fingers with his. His breath reminded me of The
Stink. In the low thick foreign voice he shares with
his twin he said longingly, 'You know . . . creating a
beautiful race. It could have been . . . Jews keep
themselves to themselves too. People should stick to
their own.' He laughed and touched my hair.

Looking at your picture he said, 'He didn't invent anti-Semitism – he was a vegetarian!' We laughed together. 'Adored by children and dogs,' he added.

'A chocolate addict!' I said.

Up this close I could see the faint telephone-number tattoo stamped on his shaved neck.

'That's a great face,' he said, touching my cheek. 'If I'd had a face like that . . .'

The phone rang three times then stopped. He shrugged. We waited for it to start up again.

That first night the Count's culinary brother served us from a cauldron of googh in our intimate red and gold room which seemed even smaller with three bodies in it. Their two Polish bodies and my Aryan body. And the three different smells that leak from our pores.

And all that food! The sight of it made me dizzy.

The vermilion chicken, the terracotta stew, the vividly multi-coloured vegetables pumped up with preservatives then bludgeoned into unnatural shapes.

Bobbie's efforts looked professional, smelled like him, and made me long to throw up as soon as I swallowed the first mouthful. When I caught him staring at me he lowered his eyes and left the room.

The Count dipped the silver serving spoon in the stew again enthusiastically.

'Not for me,' I said, preventing him from showering my plate with more gunge.

He pushed my hand aside, and said, 'So-phi-ra, you must eat,' piling it high. 'You have to eat.' I stared out the window.

His brother brought him another boulder of bread then hovered dangerously close to my back ready to serve dessert. Stacked on the dresser the monumental cake with the sick message and a pastry mountain of raspberry turnovers and a monstrous sponge covered with icing blacker than the Count's remaining bit of hair were waiting to be gobbled up.

'Sophira,' he said, stuffing meat into his entirely adorable jaws, 'you're not eating?' His eyebrows drew together.

'I'm not hungry.' I moved the poison across my plate with my silver fork. With my other hand I sprayed Blue Dew under the table.

'Perhaps you'd like to see Doctor Humphrey?'

It's beyond funny! I know why I don't eat. I'm in love! It's *normal* not to eat when you're young and in that condition.

The phone rang. He trotted through to his bedroom.

His brother called after him indulgently, 'Finish your food first!' Bobbie shook his head and said to me, 'You know, if these del-ee-cious demos keep up, Lou will make another fortune for us from this 'itler movie.'

I went over to the window and stared at the traffic

bombing down Park Lane. He was reflected behind me watching my back.

There was nobody outside.

'Lou's the clever one,' he said.

When he followed Fat into his room and closed the door I ran to Bishop Place cemetery and sat in the dark resting my back against the Riefenstahl tomb. The eagle's head was cracked. It looked as if someone with a very hard hand had punched it as a prelude to beating its brains out then changed his mind.

Passion has to be hopeless. You can't have passion that isn't hopeless. Hope ruins passion.

I'm the beautiful one, the thin white girl, the obsession. He's the embarrassment, the fat old man. This secret love can't go on.

Can the cook see me down here from his kitchen window? He's not in his kitchen. He's sitting close to Fat, plotting my downfall. Don't allow vanity to help me slide into the trap of underestimating an ugly middle-aged rival. He has the advantages of blood, history, habit.

The air here is more pure. It allows me to think. I have to do something, now, quickly, before I'm seventeen, before it's too late.

There's a teeny stone lying flat across the earth behind the Riefenstahls'. I never noticed it before. The stone is an at-a-glance guide to the size and wealth of the corpse below. This rich baby's is smooth white marble. She's been dead for a long time.

Serial killers get it all wrong. For maximum publicity they must stop rumpy-pumpying blondes and concentrate on smothering random babies parked outside shops in Churchills with hand-embroidered lace pillows. When a baby dies it's always a tragedy in the tabloids.

A boot crunched across the grass then stopped. His thin shadow was visible behind the ruined Chapel.

It's him! He's standing in the dark watching my tears. It could be anyone. I'm hopeful, scared.

His shadow moved towards me.

'Good evening, Miss.' Disappointed again.

'Hello,' I said to the crazy harmless grave-digger.

'I've seen you here before.'

'I haven't seen you.' What a liar!

'You always sit at the same one.'

I nodded. He was dressed in rags. Looking at him was freezing me. He held out his hand.

'By the way, I'm Charles Fox-Pitt – with two t's – I'm in charge here.'

'Sophira Van Ness.'

'They designed it themselves before they died.'

'Huh?'

'The Riefenstahls.' He nodded at the glowing marble eagle. 'It has lots of visitors.'

We lapsed into silence. Charles Fox-Pitt was uncomfortable.

'They died together in Bavaria on their honeymoon then were shipped back here.'

'What killed them?' Two German war criminals in

love with salvation. They ran away from retribution, sailed to the island to hide.

'Who knows,' the old man said, stuffing his hands into his pockets.

'Did they have any children?' One of his boots wasn't laced up. The wind was flapping the fake leather tongue against his skinny ankle. His flesh reminded me of Bobbie's chicken.

'There must have been children,' he said, 'to inherit all that wealth . . .'

When I stood up to go he put his hand out but didn't touch me. 'You'll be back?'

'They were English,' he called after me. 'They must have been English!'

The tramp can't read. This German doctor's wife definitely died a couple of months ago. A victim? A beast? Her husband died in 1946. Exhausted by their narrow escape? Who cares now.

As fast as possible I ran home and up all the stairs. Bobbie caught me on my way in. He must have smelled me coming or heard my wee feet. Or he was waiting behind the front door!

He glared at me saying nothing. I stared him out. He went into his kitchen and hunched over the sink scouring pots.

The Count was sitting in his red chair. His face was dry and bright and smiling at me.

'So-phi-ra,' he said. 'Where have you been?'

'Out.'

I kicked my shoes off and sat on the pale blue satin

sofa with my feet under my bum. He gulped down the remains in his glass then poured out two measures from a decanter of Eastern European cocktail. It was the colour of something foul and dead that you force yourself to drink in a dream to prove you can.

My eyes, in the window behind his head, betrayed my weakness. Casually glancing at me he said, 'Robert has promised to look after you during the day.' Our fingers brushed when he handed me my glass.

'What do you mean?' Just one sip for bravery.

'To see that you . . .' he broke off, smiling, 'to make sure you're a good Sophira.'

He laughed, I laughed. Our eyes met, my insides surged. The breaths came faster and faster. He moved over to where I was sitting.

Bobbie barged in without knocking. His wig was tousled, as if he'd been bending to the keyhole.

He said, 'Don't forget, Lou, you have to go back out tonight . . .'

Fat's face wobbled. 'Thank you, Robert,' he said, and disappeared to the bathroom. Twenty minutes later he called Goodbye to his twin and left the flat.

After watching the news to see if there was anything about you I went to bed and listened in the dark for the fat man I loved to come back, checking the time regularly on Napoleon's watch.

Just after midnight the front door opened. The twin was waiting in his kitchen.

'What, still working?' Fat called out jovially. Bobbie chuckled. Laughter embarrasses me.

They had a short conversation. I couldn't hear exactly what was said. When they'd finished talking the fat Count went straight to his room.

After Bobbie the Jobbie's arrival in Park Lane I was no longer disturbed in the morning by a demand for a deep kiss. Instead Fat sat on his toi while his twin puffed perfume and planned his day in his raw voice before packing him off to the mysterious office then shutting himself in his kitchen.

Every day he was in there whistling his brother's tunes while battering pastry, crushing sugar to death in a machine, splicing fruit into millions of little bits, beating the brains out of animal flesh to turn into another barbarian goulash. Except on Thursday mornings when he locked his bedroom door and went out to fetch supplies from shops that don't deliver.

During the day I stayed in my room until late afternoon then went out to a movie, to the Riefenstahl grave, The Eagle cafe, anywhere.

When almost time for the Count's return to Park Lane I dashed back ahead of him so that I was in the little sitting-room with really red lips when he stuck his big smiling face round the door and said in his spiritual voice, 'So-phi-ra, how are you?'

He relieved himself then came back and sat opposite me at the table. The brother served dinner then left us for a little while. Fat ate his all up, I shovelled mine across the plate wondering what to do: about being in love, about my stigmata which were becoming bigger and bigger and redder and redder, and this whole life thing.

Love is hopeless. Everything is hopeless.

The Count often had to go out in the evenings too now. He didn't say where, I didn't ask. Concealing my tortured heart was the only hope left for me.

But he started turning up at odd moments during the day. While I was in my bath I'd hear him whispering with his brother.

Or I'd come home breathless after running all the way from Bishop Place and he'd be on the phone giving orders to his office in his aggressive but charming voice. He suits phones. He suits his big black car. He doesn't suit being a twin.

He concentrates really hard when he's on the phone. Sometimes he doesn't see me standing in the unlit corridor behind him.

But I don't mind the one I love's distractions. Because if there's one thing worse than loving a fat man it's if he ever finds out: you're in his power for life.

He could make you do degrading things. Tell you to hold his fat hand in public. Limit you to one bath a day. Force you to give up chocolate!

Would I have fallen madly in love with this fat

man if Jack hadn't disappeared? I hate Jack. He'll be sorry.

What will I do when I'm old? Should I tell the Count that on 20th April it's my seventeenth birthday? What age would you be now beloved Adolf if you hadn't been forced to die in an unholy blaze of glory? You'd be a very old man. I love old men. You'd be older than my dead grandfather.

The sum of the rivals is constant, mother used to say, hunched in front of her mirror applying black mascara to her sunken screwed up eyes, a cigarette burning. Her rivals were younger, thinner, brighter blondes.

My rival never goes out.

The opportunity to see inside Bobbie's bedroom didn't come until the last Thursday morning in March when he went food shopping without locking his door.

I wasn't looking for anything, just looking. That made the photographs all the more of a shock. But there can be simple explanations for massive coincidences.

Usually I sleep through the cook's weekly forays to the outside world, Thursday's just another day for me. When I wake up he's back, the freezer's loaded, I take my bath and go out.

But I'd been up all night fretting about Fat, and my

approaching birthday, and the stigmata. The marks were even bigger. Blue Dew was doing nothing for it. The edges were swollen, inflamed, *ugly*. Midnight sweats were causing my matted fringe to stick to the bloody crosses.

Last night he tried to touch me. He came in late, I was standing in the dark in the hallway thinking: here I am in a ridiculous situation with a fat man who's obsessed with his brother's cooking. It isn't a situation, it's a broken heart. It's outrageous. I should run away, rob an off-licence, never see him again. Or force him to reinstate the ritual morning kiss.

People say, *You won't always feel like this*. But the unbearable bit is knowing that's true. Emotions don't endure. You can't control them. They disappear tomorrow then torment you again next year. It doesn't last forever, it repeats itself.

I always think, *Why didn't they* or *She should have* or *Why couldn't he* . . . I want them even in my imagination to stick to their imperatives, fix their lives. The daydream must be clean. The movie perfect. The hope intact, secretly.

He walked towards me. I could smell him. To taste his sweat I'd give up my red Chinese dress.

He closed in. His face looks different. He's done something to his face.

'So-phi-ra,' he whispered. 'So-phi-ra . . .'

'Don't touch me!' I screamed. 'Don't you ever touch me.'

His grey face wobbled. Making him suffer could cure me. It's my only hope.

The key turned in Bobbie's lock. He appeared in the dusky hallway in his brown corduroy robe. He's naked underneath it. He pulled it closer to his body, smiling.

The Count turned away from me. His trousers looked loose from behind. His solidity's a masquerade. It convinced everyone including me. But now he isn't a really really fat man! He is marked out by his clothes and expression and folds of his skin as a man who used to be impressively fat and is now just plain old fat.

They exchanged a wordless look. Bobbie's eyes were saying, 'I told you that girl eez craz-ee.'

The phone rang. Fat picked it up.

'Nobody there,' he said helplessly, replacing the receiver. He stood staring at the phone.

He didn't follow me into my room. I lay with the covers pulled up to just under my eyes. Electric light in the air, the mirror, the door. Dark outside. Traffic. My favourite time is midnight.

I switched the light off, went back under.

After all I want his arms in the dark. I don't want to long for him. I feel ridiculous but need to be safe forever in his heavy arms with their smell and his dense chest and all the things he said in the beginning, the things a fat man with an accent can say without sounding silly, the sort of declarations that would ruin a thin man.

Run now, throw yourself into his bed?

Fear is the greatest sin. Jack despises cowards.

*

Eventually I will fall asleep and when I wake up it will all be fixed. That's dying.

The past can be rewritten. Change the end. You created a new war because the first score didn't satisfy you. You did the things other men fantasise. The glamorous prefer death to failure and die in spiritual glory.

But this burden of never completely forgetting that makes me the same as everyone else. I like Chinese clothes, I love the dark, imagining my own best self. I want everything to be perfect forever with my eyes the colour they were at Berchtesgaden: sharp bright blue under the clouds like yours. Because the weak are always wrong, and traitors have to die, and England is an island where the fat die young.

To be brave forever and offered your arms and say No. I can wait, imagining everything. Death for betrayal.

Create a master plan not later now. Triumph. Will it to happen. Demolish rivals. God has a headstart in bastardhood. We'll never catch up with Him. But you will always be Germany's beloved Adolf the humane hero of Berchtesgaden. The children who brought blue flowers to the Berghof have grown and invented new children who spit on the renamed USA Strasse. They call it Beloved Adolf Strasse. They worship you. You were the best thing that ever happened to Germany. When a love affair ends badly we still long for the lover.

You were murdered by insanely jealous rivals in the unholy world then immortalised by their hatred.

History labours round the clock to discredit you but you survive, you become more sexy. You're the world's immortal fantasy.

I ran to the window, you weren't outside.

Go to the mirror. Don't switch on the light.

Changed my mind. Can't face the stigmata in this mood.

I went back to bed and lay on top of the covers sweating. There wasn't a sound from his room. The lights in the hall were out. My left eye was throbbing. Crying would make it worse. Even the traffic in Park Lane was diminishing. London closes at midnight, earlier. My left eye is different from my right eye, I'm a surreal Nefertiti, I'm winning.

I went back to the mirror for another thirteen minutes then ran back to bed.

Just as I was drifting off the answer came, typical when there's no pen, and this was such a solution . . .! By morning I'll have forgotten. I considered fumbling in the dark for something to write with but drifted off, waking with that puzzled feeling of loss when I heard the outside door slam.

He's left a fresh shit stain in our toilet. I smelled it, pleased, went into his room, picked up his discarded boxers. The connecting door into his brother's bedroom was open. He forgot to lock it!

But what if he's in there? I couldn't bring myself to call out his name.

*

The whiff inside his room was overpowering. I sank back against the wall. It stank like a middle-aged woman's unwashed jobbie-hole.

His corduroy bathrobe was discarded on the floor by the unmade bed. The chair was covered with soiled unisex bloomers. A succession of shapeless brown outfits lined the wardrobe. There was nothing under the bed except smelly coils of black rubber hose.

The mouldy smell was even worse in his bathroom. A Chinese vase of badly arranged blue flowers was sitting on the toilet beside a lidless tube of depilatory cream. A greasy bottle of cheap detergent shampoo with a cluster of coarse synthetic hairs at its neck was perched on the edge of the bath with the lid off. One little push would topple it.

I looked at myself in his mirror. The sleeping fucking beauty.

The lift doors closed. I listened for the key in the lock. He can't be finished shopping already.

A full minute. Nothing. It's the one I love! That was my secret thought, the one I couldn't think out loud.

Another minute passed without a sound. Really it's no one.

Watching the door in the mirror I opened the top and bottom drawers of his dresser. Looking for what? There was only what you'd expect to find amongst the possessions of a bony middle-aged ghoul. A plain man with a dirty nose who can cook scoff the Count *loves*. A refugee from you, beloved one, with kosher experience. An escapee of Dr Riefenstahl's research programme – for all the good it did, he would have looked better as a lampshade.

I stuck my hand under his mattress. Nothing. On his bedside table there's a gilt-framed photograph of Fat looking extra fat.

What am I afraid of? That he'll be happy? That I've lost something? That he won't be miserable for the rest of his life without me?

Crammed in Bobbie's drawer were millions of pictures of the actor playing you in the Count's movie. He looks like you, beloved Adolf. Cute haircut, sharp cheekbones, eccentric hands. He's standing in his leather coat on a monumental platform in the distance, hat low, his anachronistic leather sunglasses turned from the camera. A vulnerable indestructible impersonation of a photogenic dog-lover whose intentions were misunderstood.

He looks like Jack.

Under the photographs there was a plan of the set. It has a real underground bunker exactly like yours, the one they destroyed. Clipped to this sketch was a psychotically folded map – A Quick Route from London to Berlin – with a train timetable. I put the map in my jammie pocket.

At the very back of the drawer I found the snap of the grave. The picture was taken at night, the flash obscuring the name engraved in the stone, but the eagle on top is unmistakable. It's the Riefenstahl grave. Jack's photograph?

How could Jack possibly know an ugly Jewish

man? Maybe Bobbie likes the eagle too? This picture was taken before its head cracked.

The front door opened. I heard Bobbie go into the kitchen, lift the freezer lid.

There's time to escape.

Why should I?

He paused in the hallway outside his bedroom door before inserting the key, turning it, pushing. I wanted him to run in brandishing one of his knives, to finish it for good. A kill or be killed situation.

'Attack first,' Mother used to say, hunched over her make-up mirror preparing for a manhunt.

Bobbie slithered in giggling and sank down on his bed, pushing the brown coat open with his knees. His legs were covered in almost invisible nylon stockings.

'Lou ought to help me with that load,' he said, stretching, exposing a fleshless thigh, adding slyly, 'he's the one who eats.'

He gave me his idea of a flirtatious smile. 'So-phi-ra,' he said, sounding like the Count, 'you're so white!'

I went to the kitchen and poured a bowl of krispies and sat at the scrubbed wooden table. He followed me through. As I dug my spoon in, the chocolate lumps overflowed. I munched away; he stared out at the cemetery muttering, 'A woman we used to know was just buried down there.'

I'd rather die than ask. What's it to me if the

slasher killed Frau Riefenstahl or if her medical husband was ever involved in the devil's research?

'You're wasting your time here,' Bobbie said.

I heaped my plate with cereal. Don't rot your soul with doubt. We're in love with death until it's too late.

'With a face like that . . .' He shrugged. 'You could go anywhere . . . Prague, Berlin. You could be in the mov-ees.' He laughed. I laughed. He crossed his legs.

'One thing is sure – Lou doesn't need company.'

He hunched his bony back over the *Stab*. I was dying to see if you were mentioned, but controlled myself. I can buy my own copy when I go to the cinema.

The phone rang. He grabbed it, made a face, dropped the receiver, muttered sulkily, 'Mr Nobody again.'

When I'd finished munching he said, 'You'd better get that boil on your face lanced . . .'

But it didn't work, I didn't care, my mind was made up.

I took my time getting dressed, checked the listings (*Killer's Kiss* at the Ritz, it's my lucky day!), hid the map of Berlin in the lining of my jacket then called out, 'Goodbye Robert,' before slamming the front door.

I'm going to seduce the fat bastard Count tonight or make them both sorry.

*

All through the film I imagined it.

I left the Ritz at six just after the movie started playing again and wandered around damp Soho streets and saw a pair of gloves gloomily lit in a closed shop's window. They're motorcycle leather and cost fifty-five pounds. The shop door had a handwritten sign stuck on with black tape saying, 'Back in five.'

After checking behind me I wandered into The Eagle and sat in my window seat and ordered hot chocolate. There was no one outside that I could see. I hope it rains later. I started thinking about it again.

Tonight when he's asleep I'll climb into bed beside the massive dark shape. The big blubbery body may not be quite as heavy as it looks when it rolls on top of me. The smell will be familiar. His body's always doused in sweat, unforgettably oozing through his pores mingling with the scent of his perfume. His bed's a hothouse. No matter what, he keeps himself covered. I've imagined the flesh smothering me but never seen it all.

Tomorrow morning we'll be twin souls. Bobbie can like it or lump it, as Old Gorm would say.

By six-forty I'd already begun to think about going home, dealing with destiny. He could be sitting waiting for his feed in the small hot dimly-lit room already.

A blond came in just as my drink arrived. He was watching himself in the fake eighteenth-century whorehouse mirror behind my head. Twenty-four, tall, but with short legs. He sat down opposite me.

Have you ever noticed that men with short legs usually have broad noses too? No matter what they wear they look untidy.

You always look clean, beloved Adolf, in your entirely adorable uniforms.

The coffee in this fool's cup was like a brown puddle. When he leaned forward to drink the filth his elbows made the table vibrate, shaking the stained glass lamp between his half and mine. He kept fucking smiling at me. His teeth hadn't been cleaned since yesterday. The fingers of my right hand were tapping my neck where my rosary used to be and my face was shaking.

I reached over to the next table and grabbed a *Stab*.

Someone wants to resurrect the death penalty. Prince Charles is frothing at the mouth.

Some fucking pink lefties are pictured holding another fucking demo about your birthday. Your big day's my big day, don't remind me, it's coming soon. The pinkos want us all to sign their petition. I don't have anything against them I just couldn't eat a whole one, Napoleon used to say.

The blond was smiling at himself in the mirror behind me. Why didn't I sit facing that way?

It was impossible to watch his cup any longer. Maybe I should go back and buy those gloves. Someone else came in. The blond was attempting to scratch himself under the table. He's a heroin addict. He stood up then sat back down again. When the Count sits on his gold toi his flesh all bunches up. When he's lying down it's worse because you never know when it will wobble in your direction. That's what I used to pretend.

A skin formed on top of my hot chocolate. I went downstairs to the toilet and washed my hands then stood in the dark listening. He could come up behind me any minute. He could have been waiting for an opportunity all this time.

Back upstairs I ordered a lemonade with a straw. The straw is an old habit inherited from Jack. The blond had left. After swallowing most of the lemonade very quickly I moved back to my window seat but sat facing the mirror this time. The blond had attempted some clues in the *Stab* crossword. People who do that make me sick.

I sat watching workers hurry along the street thinking, *As soon as the rush is over I'll grab a taxi,* when something disagreeable happened. Someone I know passed right by my window! I stuck my face in the *Stab*, staring at a piece about US culture. Americans can be jungle bunnies or slavs or geeks and no one cares. They're all equal in the melting pot, one nation under God, freedom, liberty and wacky baccie for all. Sieg Heil.

The door jingle jangled and I knew it was him coming in – the jessie biscuit slave with the pocked skin, yellow hair and mad red eyes who serves Her Majesty.

'Sophira!' Nylon screeched. 'I can't believe it's really you.' He ran towards me, one arm outstretched, the other lugging an overstuffed briefcase. I backed into the wall.

He's grown a gay moustache, is suffering from an incurable disease, and his skin hasn't improved with age.

'This is radical, Honey,' he said, then sat down and burst out crying. A green line of snot dangled between his left nostril and top lip as his mouth worked furiously for control. The tears were blinding him.

He spluttered, 'My eyes are going to be ruined.'

'Look, I have to go,' I said, standing up.

'Sophira! You can't leave me like this . . . I've been looking for you for weeks – you're practically my best friend, my last hope, the only one who can save me . . . Tell me what to do. I beg you!' He clung to my arm blubbering. I stared at the blood spattered on his collar and sat back down, loosening his grip. I mopped my brow with a crumpled piece of napkin.

'My God! Your face . . .' He gaped at me. I shook my fringe over the stigmata, laughing, eyes bright.

He shifted in his chair, embarrassed, asked me what I wanted to drink.

'Nothing, I really have to go . . .'

'Have you seen Jack?' he asked, stalling.

'No . . .' He was trembling. Maybe he knows something?

'Have you?'

'Me?'

He started whimpering again. 'I don't want to be left,' he said. 'Bill's a slut but I love him . . . He'll kill me if I blow it . . . I don't want to be left . . . He's going to be bigger than the Nuremberg Rallies.'

'Huh?'

He dug into his briefcase and pulled out a wad of prints, sifting through them until he came to a blonde woman with thinner legs and bluer eyes than me. She has clear polish on her short rounded fingernails, she's a fine Aryan specimen.

'It's Eva Braun,' he blurted, breaking down again. I went to the bar and fetched two coffees, filled his cup with sugar and stuck it under his face then waited for him to fini.

The waiter put Bach on the juke box. My foot tapped invisible, noiseless, under the table. People with problems nauseate me.

Twelve minutes later Nylon's swollen face settled and he told me his story.

Bill the black butler gave up butlering when he fucked himself into a part as a token black in the Third Reich. And it might be serious, he could be *on the turn*, seeing a *woman* – this Eva slut who doesn't look a bit like the real Mrs Hitler. Who, on closer inspection of the photograph, isn't more attractive than me at all. And she looks at least twenty-four, though she could be a badly preserved twenty-two.

He hardly ever sees black Bill – he's on set all hours (thank *Heaven* the movie's almost fini) and Nylon's at the Palace from sunrise 'til late (today's his day off – the first since last year) and what will happen next?

He can't go on living like this, he deserves *alimony* if he's going to be left.

I asked to see more pictures. He handed me a folder full of Bill – in black and white, black and colour, clothed, nude, erect, hanging loose.

'Have you any pictures of Hitler?'

Nylon blushed, shrugged, stared at the glass lampshade.

'He doesn't allow his photograph to be taken. He's fanatical about it – unless he's being paid.'

He dug in his bag and proudly produced a map, the same as the one hidden in my pocket. 'You can have this,' he said. 'I've got two.'

'Thanks.'

'I'm not afraid to face it,' he said, bottom lip quivering, a hurt orphanic pleading look in his red eyes. 'I'm definitely going to do it.'

'Do what?'

'Confront them. We should go out there and sort it out once and for all. Invade that bunker if we have to. Take the first train out there – well, first thing tomorrow afternoon . . . It's best to know, isn't it?'

'Storm the set,' I said, 'you're doing the right thing,' standing decisively, smiling at myself in the mirror, making it to the door.

'Sophira – you can't *go*! You haven't touched your drink.' The door jingled. He covered his mouth with his hand, blurting, 'I'm making a right mess of everything . . .'

'Goodbye, Bryan,' I called vivaciously, marching into the darkness.

There wasn't an empty taxi in sight. I can't fucking drive, I have to rely on taxis, and worry the whole time about who would drive the getaway car.

Walking the damp dark streets all the way home I thought about Fat, about how I would do it straight away, as soon as I see him. A miraculous triumph.

I thought about the slasher too, imagined him behind me, wondered what's keeping him away from slashing for so long. He's a smart killer, he's found another thrill. They'll never catch him. He's invented a new mad bad game for the spiritually reckless. He's impersonating you, beloved Adolf, challenging your soul, changing your destiny.

Two Chinese boys came out of our building as I was going in. The youngest held the door open for me.

I didn't have to share the lift with anyone which seemed good fate but as soon as I opened our front door I knew.

Unattended sizzling noises spurted out of the kitchen. Bobbie wasn't guarding his pots. In all the time I've known him he's never gone to the bathroom in the middle of cooking. He doesn't let the grub out of his sight until his brother, the large love of our lives, has shovelled it down his fat neck.

I removed my shoes and tiptoed into our bathroom. The marble chilled my wee feet. I'll catch my death, as the old slave Gorm used to say. But she's not a slave anymore, she's living secluded at The Haugh while I'm here in filthy old London.

*

The low regular sound was definitely coming from his bed. The smell of his shit floated through the door when I kicked it open with my toe.

The Count was face down sobbing into the mattress. His hairy arms were tied with rubber hose to the bedposts above his head. Someone had propped his pelvis up on pillows to project his blubbery behind upwards.

This is the first time I've seen his whole bare bum. I'm glad the light's dim but know that somewhere, hidden in the folds of soft flesh, is the hole where his jobbies emerge from.

The wrenching sobs became calmer. With effort he lifted his face and murmured, 'I beg you,' in the accent I'd decided to love.

He twisted his head in my direction then screwed his eyes tightly shut like a stupid child who thinks you can't see it when it can't see you.

Bobbie came into the room unbuttoning his brown coat as he approached the bed. He smiled triumphantly at me, threw his coat on the floor and climbed on his brother's back.

I want to die. I want to kill.

'You want this,' he said prising Fat's buttocks open, pressing his front against his twin's behind.

The rolls of flesh strained apart.

'I beg you,' the Count said. 'I beg you.'

The smell was unbearable.

'Lie still,' his brother whispered soothingly.

Without disturbing his thrust Bobbie turned his

head and said to me, 'Dinner won't be long, So-phi-ra.'

As I left the flat the phone started ringing. Running downstairs I could still hear it.

Outside under the portico I hesitated. Which direction? A moist grey-blue starlight, the air sharp but not unclean and it's essential to make the right choice. Left or right? Storm the set. Audition for a part in that movie.

Never forgive a traitor. Don't compromise an ideal. Most of the misery in the world is caused by mistaking weak men for strong. All along it should have been myself not the fantasy of finding someone braver.

As I walked to the station my head was aching, I had about five pounds in change and was determined not to count it. The drizzle started, I became Tamara de Lempicka melting in the rain on the road to reinvented Berlin.

BOOK III
The Final Solution

'If I wish it I obtain it.'

SIMONE WEIL

My sheets were damp when I woke in the bunker calling for you. The candles were still glowing but I knew it was morning because a Holy Grail goblet of lemonade and crystal dish of jelly babies had appeared by your ascetic bed.

I was still dazed enough to wonder if it was true, if you had really sat watching me all night in the erect red swastika chair below the portrait of your hero Frederick the Great.

My matted hair had been pinned back and pus from the burst stigmata was oozing down my forehead onto the collar of your Bavarian blue and white striped jammies. Blue's our colour.

Everything became clear. It's you or me. A kill or be killed situation.

Last night when I arrived at the movie set I ran down Unter den Linden and climbed straight into the bunker, wedging a brick in the concrete lid, aware that it wouldn't do any damn good against Providence.

My face tangled in a fake spider's web as I jumped from step to step down the steep narrow spiral into a gloomy golden hallway. Reading the inspiring advice carved into the walls – Our Honour is Our Loyalty, Death for Betrayal, What we must Fight for is the Purity of our Blood – I tripped over a Japanese camera and a set of spotlights then kicked an empty lemonade tin along the L-shaped candlelit corridor to your rooms at the end.

I'd have to be stupid not to know it was you all along: standing across the street watching the Count's building, calling without speaking, appearing in all those newspapers in adored Adolf's uniform.

Outside the war room there was a length of strangler's string and a heap of rags bundled over something.

My black boot left an imprint on the door when I kicked it open.

Sitting in front of the party flag, you're staring at an immense screen, examining your rushes.

Feverishly damp, stigmata throbbing, I sat down beside you. You re-ran the rally:

The SS motorcade cuts through your disciplined mob of extras. You jump from your black Mercedes: heroic, clean, invulnerable. You must know the meaning of death at least as you salute firmly, shrug your leather greatcoat from your shoulders, shake the unruly silk lock from your forehead and take your place on the platform at the centre of destiny.

Your worshippers cheer themselves into oblivion. You raise your hand. There's a silence while you flick back your fringe, pause, then begin your calculated speech inciting us all to a triumph of your will.

We must eliminate your enemies. We are the master race. You are the master. There's only ever one of you per bunker. It is preordained.

The frantic crowd with their spiritual expressions are ready to die for you. Their hearts are closed to pity. They know the strongest man is right, the weak are always wrong.

You are all-powerful. Faces tremble when you are mentioned. Sacred monster, by yourself you reinvented the world. You forced millions to choose death. And after your war women were no longer fitted for underwear: hand-stitched, silk, monogrammed. Everything decayed after your purity.

But you failed, eternally impotent Adolf. You conquered a continent then lost interest in glory. You needed an audience to die.

Grandfather told Donald and me as we rocked his chair, 'You always get what you want.' People afraid of wanting too much betray themselves.

And now, my uncorrupted darling, crazy Aryan genius, psychotic God: you're a joke, a travesty, an apologetic icon, the media star of every genocidal melodrama, every military farce. You're all things to all men.

The adoring mob haven't noticed this man isn't you. It's a live version of a dead God they're paid by the Count to take seriously. It's Jack dressed up as you. He's a thrill a minute and he has blue eyes. His spirit is strong, he's earning more money than anyone in this movie.

*

'Sophira,' you said, 'you look sleepy,' and led me into your minimalist bedroom.

My crucifix and your black padded leather gloves were on top of your desk.

'You're the slasher,' I said, pressing my fingers against my forehead.

'I have a talent for death,' you said, smiling, then you kissed my stigmata and changed me into your jammies. I hesitated before climbing into the narrow iron bed. You picked up my crucifix, draped it round my neck, kissed my stigmata again.

I lay clutching Christ under the starched white sheets. You tucked me in tight then sat down on the red chair, shoulders back, head high.

'Sophira,' you said, 'my Prussian Princess. That bed suits you. You have the bluest eyes . . . the whitest skin – whiter than Heaven. Ah, Sophira, there's never been a blue like the blue of your eyes. There's an aura of blue around you, an aura of purity . . . a feeling of doom.'

At first the inscription on the back of my crucifix looked like a scratch from my longest fingernail which is ragged but impossible to give up. But when I held it closer to the gold flame I saw it clearly: *Death for Betrayal*.

A sudden thick smell made me sit up. After that I had fallen into Nod until this silence woke me at the crack of dawn.

I stumbled into the corridor, kicked all the doors. Every one was locked except the war room. I should have asked for the bathroom last night.

The hatch at the top of the narrow stairs was slightly ajar. Daylight mingled with the yellowish-cream glow of wax. The faked Old Masters lining the staircase evoked an aura of puritanical decadence that could only work in a movie.

My wee feet were almost too big for the narrow steps as I climbed up, avoiding the chewing gum web, closing in on daylight. I was sweating, heart pounding, using my full strength to force the bunker's concrete lid all the way up.

Sunlight immediately attacked me. The deserted celluloid city reinforced with steel was a mix of forties Berlin and Paris. Down Unter den Linden, past the Brandenburg Gate, beyond the uninhabited Tiergarten a trail of dead blue flowers was abandoned on the grass.

I climbed the Chancellery steps for a better view of the adjoining set. Leaning against a flimsy Tour Eiffel abandoned on its side next to a bust of Frederick the Great I watched the monumental Speeresque platform waiting for you on the horizon.

It's not my destiny to wait.

As I was marching out of Berlin his Mercedes convertible pulled up alongside me. I climbed in. His big wheels cut a path through blue flowers and discarded swastika flags, passing through the gates and following the curve of dust and industry to the main road. The fingers of Jack's left hand drummed the dash energetically, spasmodically bursting into machine-gunfire. From time to time he slugged from a can of lemonade, offering it to me even though he knew I would say No.

The sun's beating down on me, he's driving faster and faster. He wants me to lie on the floor and cover my eyes.

'The brakes are weak.'

The thrill of fear made me smile. Bravery is unpremeditated. Invulnerability is a good thing. It would kill me if he wasn't perfect.

'Go faster.'

Suddenly the rain started. He had no intention of putting up the roof. I held my face up to cleanse the stigmata. The wound has started to close already. My rosary's back where it belongs around my neck and soon I'll be safe forever.

'How's the Count?' Jack had always known I would betray him. He expected it of me. The disappointment would've killed him if I hadn't.

'How's Eva?'

We fell into violent silence, occasionally emitting subdued laughter.

When we entered dead early morning London he asked where I was going.

'Berchtesgaden.'

He raised his arm in salute. 'Beautiful country, I had a house there once.' Jack laughed his mad laugh, I joined in, he pulled up outside Fat's building. We didn't say Goodbye.

When he disappeared I ran up Park Lane to Marble Arch and stood in the doorway of the synagogue watching my old room in the Royal Hotel. The blind was lowered to the level I used to leave it when I was lying on my back on the floor watching footsteps.

Twelve minutes later by Napoleon's watch I went into reception to use the payphone. There was a new thirty year old on the desk. I couldn't see P.D., but was feeling reckless, didn't care about being recognised.

Fat's phone rang twice then jessie Bob answered. He must have been passing it in the hallway. When I asked if I was in Bobbie said, 'She's not here now,' and hung up.

'I know,' I said, replacing the receiver.

It's too late. You can never go back once something's desecrated.

Mother's phone rang for ages before she picked it up.

'Hello,' she said huskily.

'Hello.'

'It's you! You woke us up. How did you know I was back?'

'I guessed.'

'How did you get this number?'

'The operator.'

'I haven't seen you for ages.'

'I know.' There was a silence. Five seconds? Ten? It feels longer on the phone.

'What're you up to?'

'Nothing much.' Another pause. 'How are you?'

'As ever,' she said jauntily. She sucked on her cigarette. 'You know me! Happy as Larry.' Happiness is for failures.

Out of the blue, as I was trying to think up something else to say, she asked: 'Do you ever think of *him*?'

'What?'

For a minute I thought she meant Jack.

'You *know* . . .'

My throat closed off and I scrunched down, pressing my head into the wall and said too fast, 'Look I must go I'm using someone else's phone.' We both knew I was lying.

'Well it was good hearing from you, drop us a line sometime.'

'Bye,' I said.

'Bye,' she replied. 'Keep in touch!'

She started to say something else, either to me or a person in her new house. When I pressed the follow-on call button I still had credit.

I dialled her number again. A man's voice said, 'Hello?'

'Hello,' he said again. This time I knew it was Uncle Ned.

There's only one solution now: fulfil my own destiny, execute my will, reclaim my inheritance.

When I opened my eyes at The Haugh the window was flung wide. Fresh air billowed the curtains but the overpowering presence of blue roses still filled Napoleon's room. A large Chinese vase crammed with them was reflected in the mirror above the raging fire. The portrait of the real Napoleon confronted me on the wall opposite my dead grandfather's bed.

Gorm gave me the dented silver tray with a jug of homemade raspberry cordial and an overflowing bowl of chocolate krispies then hovered.

'I see you decided to wake up,' she said, creaking closer. 'Look at the state of they sheets . . .' The last of the stigmata pus had oozed onto Napoleon's starched white bed linen.

'I had to cut that herr of yours,' she said with satisfaction.

She's ruined my fringe. What do I want with a blinding fringe?

'How long have I been asleep?'

'It's Tuesday today,' she said, 'work it oot for yoursell. But we haven't had a mess like that since he died.' She pointed her bony finger at the four poster.

'He would have died in that bed if he hadn't died downstairs.'

Don and me could jump on this bed day and night if we felt like it because Napoleon was always smoking in the library and Gorm was ecstatic if we kept out of her sight.

I swished some of the red liquid around my mouth before swallowing it. 'He wouldn't have died if you hadn't set his house on fire,' I said, watching her in the mirror.

She shook her head in disgust. 'He knew his time was up.' Bending over, she picked something up off the stone floor then threw whatever it was in the fire and shuffled over to the door. Without turning round she said, 'I knew you'd be back.'

I listened for her creaking downstairs then touched my glowing face in the mirror. The stigmata've been successfully obliterated. My forehead's unstained. To sleep like the devil is obviously the answer.

Close-up those blue flowers were black. They've drunk their water and died. Propped against the vase there was a card covered with red hearts dripping blood.

I climbed back into bed, watching my reflection. I don't look my age. What's left of my hair is sprawled like Chinese silk across the starched white pillows. I could have it all cut now there's nothing to hide, but I can't risk the barber in the village. And it's almost my fucking birthday again.

*

Nothing's changed in Storm. When I arrived last week I went straight to Mass. Vampire velvet curtains, kneeling ancients, wonderful. The same twenty-two people have been attending Father Batchelor's exhortations since I was last here. Donald and I used to throw stones at them on their way in to confess. The broken pane on the extended arm of the stained glass Christ in torment on the window behind the altar still allows the rain to lash in.

When I knelt at the back near the candles of death I realised that some of the number had passed into the next world since my last cleansing and been replaced by their children. Cage the lawyer's son smiled suspiciously at me. He used to be a fat kid Don and I never allowed on our beach.

While it was all going on I fell into a doze clutching my rosary.

Jack's standing by the river at Berchtesgaden cleaning his nails. I push him. As he's falling I stab him seven times in the neck. His blood spurts down his leather coat and splashes my skin as he disappears underwater, laughing.

Dobson the butcher shook me awake. The communion line was forming along the aisle. My cheeks felt wet. I shrouded my veil around my face and whispered, 'I haven't confessed.'

He hauled me into the queue anyway. Maybe he didn't hear?

'I'm in an unclean state.'

This remark was ignored too. He was ahead of me

and his wife was behind me. As I neared the altar I saw Old Gorm creaking onto her knees. She opened her jaws and Father slung in a wafer. She smacked her martyrish downward-turning lips shut. Cage the lawyer's son helped her back up on her feet.

I couldn't believe it. What's she doing here? The shock brought me out in a sweat. She swore never to have anything more to do with this place until time for Last Rites.

She caught my eye as she backed away from the crucified son of God. Her expression was the usual blend of bitterness and satisfaction but she didn't look surprised to see me.

I spilled the blood of Christ. Someone laughed. Father Batchelor doesn't believe in complaining out loud but he knows how to whine with his eyes.

When I'd made it back to my seat I draped myself over the prayer mat. When Father came at the end of the devotions to find out why I hadn't attended for over ten years his breath made me faint.

Dobson the butcher drove me back to The Haugh while Gorm took the short cut along the beach. Dobson's wife Pearl sat in the back of the van with a carcass. I had a good view of her in the mirror from where I was lounging dangerously close to collapse in the front seat. Once a face has passed a certain stage it's had it. The van was jerking all over the place and stinking of dead cow but Pearl demanded to know what shade of lipstick I was wearing.

Of course Gorm reached The Haugh before us. The tide was well out. She was standing in the courtyard ready to haul me into the house. Her scarred stinking cat was slithering ungracefully at her big feet. You'd think it would have had the decency to die of old age by now.

'I wouldn't like to be in your shoes,' she said, staring into my eyes with her two cracked holes. 'You're like death walking.'

She didn't invite the butcher or his wife over the door. When Pearl clambered out of the van Gorm said, 'You'll be in a rush to get back for your young Sammie,' and slammed the front door in their faces.

She said to me, 'It's just the two of us here now.' It was impossible to tell if she meant me and her or her and The Stink.

She sent me to bed but Doctor Feathers wasn't disturbed until the morning. His visit alarmed me but I was too tired to run and hide in the woods like Donald and I did when we had measles and he wanted to lance our spots. Doctor told me there was nothing wrong with me and gave me something to make me sleep.

'Why did I faint?'

'You young lassies are all the same,' he said in disgust. 'Your mither used to faint – or was it yer grannie . . . You're too bloody clean that's yer trouble.' He's the double of Father Batchelor these days. It wouldn't surprise me if they're related. There's a lot of illegal breeding in these seaside villages.

Gorm ushered him out.

I spat up most of his potion and tiptoed to my door.

John-Paul Feathers was in a huddle with Gorm downstairs. She doesn't believe in doctors. What could they be talking about?

I leaned over the balcony but couldn't hear what they were saying. She was muttering as usual, and he had been pushed outside so his voice was lost in the waves before it had the chance to echo up to me.

The Stink was lurking on the half-landing outside the toi. Death *is* the only option for betrayal.

Every day I stare into my fire waiting for her to leave. A well-stacked fire burns forever. I hate a fire you keep having to add logs to and I can't bear orange flames. Pale gold and lilac are the colours I'd like to burn to death in.

I'm sick and tired of my room, lying here pretending to be asleep when she comes in with my tray, but my heart's not in roaming the woods. In the dream last night I was crying. I made a new bargain with God, something else to be desecrated when passion passes. I promised to forsake Jack, to bury him for good if He allows me to stay here forever. Because it's too late. I don't believe anymore. Nothing can make me listen.

The blue roses made me cry this morning. They never last. He sent them as a warning, I know that.

To let me know he can find me if he wants to. He could be here already, watching silently, waiting for me to give in.

There was blood on my mirror. This room and everything in it are mine. This house, the woods, the stretch of beach. No one can take them away from me. The blood turned out to be a raspberry stain.

I flicked open my razor and stabbed an overripe banana on my lunch tray. She always brings up fruit, I never eat it. She's trying to control my chocolate addiction a decade too late. It was her who started it when we were young.

The insides of the banana made me sick. The smell would have been enough. I wiped my mouth and threw the fruit into the furnace. The flames sizzled up like blue fizz. The thrill of watching something burn.

I took one bite out of a Haugh apple leaving red mouth marks on it then flung it out the window, watching it attack The Stink's back. It hissed and darted into the trees.

Gorm was meandering her way along the beach road in the direction of Storm. She must have closed the front door like a mouse.

Three o'clock by Napoleon's watch. She's gone to Mass again. What's wrong with her? She used to have as much use for the Holy Father as she does for anal masturbation and high heels.

Nothing in this house ever changes. Even the smells are the same. The blue disinfectant, the opium coming out from behind the library doors, chocolate pudd and stale cat in the kitchen. She keeps the library locked. That room hasn't been used since Napoleon died. She's hidden her will in there.

I bet the bunk beds in our old room are still made up.

I ran outside and slammed the door, running through the forest to my swing, plunging backwards and forwards sending leaves fluttering down the crumbling steps. Our old linden tree is an apple tree in real life.

How long will it stay light tonight? The tide's out, I could go down and take a look. Even after sundown Donald's name stands out. His was added last. Napoleon had his own name inscribed years in advance of his death to be sure of getting a space.

There's one place left in beside them.

On the morning of Donald's funeral Mother came into my room at the crack of dawn with a bowl of chocolate krispies. She pinched my nose between her bony fingers, spooned a few mouthfuls down my neck (which I spat up as soon as her back was turned) then got me ready in my claret coat and matching hat.

I'd wanted to wear black but Gorm had said, 'She'll look like a wee wuman cut doon.'

There was only me, Grandfather (holding my hand), Mother and Father Batchelor in the crypt that morning. Mother hadn't invited anyone from the village because of the shame of outliving your own son. Old Gorm was at home nursing The Stink – the beast was still nervous after my attack – and Uncle Neddie had missed his train up from Glasgow. But he would be coming later.

'Something for us all not to look forward to,' Napoleon said, smiling at me. He looked extra old, hunched under the damp roof of the cave.

Father Batchelor asked us to join him in a hymn of praise to the Lord but our hearts weren't in it.

Clutching my white leather bible, concentrating on not crying, I remembered: *I will never leave thee nor forsake thee*.

Donald wouldn't expect me to cry, not in front of them.

Father Batchelor was saying, 'Ashes to ashes, dust to dust,' or whatever it was, and we all went back to The Haugh for steaming hot chocolate and soggy toast Old Gorm had buttered hours before we were due to eat it.

She was back in her kitchen when I went in, huddled up close to the open stove door sucking toffees, a cold sore on the corner of her nostril. Her mouth was floating in a chipped cat-food dish up on the sink but there was no sign of the beast.

She spat into the flames. 'You're just like your grandfather.'

I fetched myself a tumbler and filled it with water from the tap. Water is God's tranquiliser. The glass smelled of Blue Dew.

'Your dinner's ruined.' Her mouth was full of toffee.

'I don't want any.'

'You're a bloody disgrace,' she said, throwing a purple wrapper into the oven. There's a pause then it flares up, dissolves, vanishes.

'It's your birthday on Tuesday,' she said cattily; her pleasantly vicious smile reminding me, against my will, of Bobbie the Jobbie.

As I was climbing the stairs she stumbled out into the hallway. I stopped on the half-landing to see what she wanted. The light wouldn't go on.

She called out something. In the dark it was difficult to tell what she was muttering. I changed my mind about looking in our old room and went straight up to the top floor.

In the middle of the night I woke up at death's door. The stench from the flowers was unbearable. I had swallowed half the water in the glass by my bed when I noticed a drowned spider stuck to the rim. Spiders are a sign money's coming.

Donald and I had a pet spider called Lucifer. We kept him in a sealed rose garden we made ourselves. He was a cannibal. But he had an affair with a female spider, Lucinda. When we dropped her into his garden instead of dismantling her to eat raw, Lucifer made friends. But when we went back to school Old Gorm starved them to death.

I spat into the fire and threw those flowers in. They killed the feeble flicker but the soggy stems stained my fingers.

My legs were weak but I had to fetch water. Outside on the landing I thought I heard a laugh. It's impossible to detect what's sickening in the laughter of others. Standing on the top step looking down made me long to jump.

Down a flight in the bathroom I made sure the stigmata weren't back then fed my mouth from the tap and splashed my sweaty face. Gorm's yellow toothbrush was standing alone in a mug on the toilet. My pocket travel toothbrush was in my cosmetic case upstairs. Can you *imagine* leaving your unprotected toothbrush on the cistern? And if you were locked in a bathroom alone with a sour taste in your mouth and knew no one was *ever* going to find out would you be tempted to use a woman with false teeth's toothbrush?

My legs were trembling as I tried to crawl back upstairs. I could just see myself shattering to dust from falling over the balcony.

Instead of hurrying back to Napoleon's bed I went along the hall to our old room. I stood outside the door and flicked my razor out. The blade pricked my throat. A red line trickled down my neck. I smeared it onto my hand, sucked it clean, held the wound. My blood is pure.

At daybreak the scarlet sky encouraged me to go

back upstairs to Napoleon's bed on time for her arrival with my tray.

In the four-poster I lay behind the curtains listening to the waves close in, wondering what was keeping her, looking forward to my cordial, finally passing into a restless sleep dreaming I was awake.

When I regained consciousness Napoleon's watch had stopped at three. My tray wasn't by the bed. The roses were still lying in the grate.

After listening at the top of the stairs I sprinted down to the kitchen for a drink of water.

The house was like death. Last night's cups were dirty in the sink. Gorm's teeth were still immersed in the old cat bowl.

The phone in the hall was off the hook. What's the point, it never rings. She has it for emergencies.

It was four o'clock, the sky was darkening, I opened the front door and stared down the drive. The wind flapped up my jammies. There wasn't a soul on the beach road.

Gorm had forgotten to lock the library doors.

The red velvet curtains were drawn, sealing in the old smell of opium. When my eyes adjusted I realised the mahogany coffin with the iron cross nailed on the lid lying on the dining-table was real. The surface was smooth. It had been polished aggressively to a high gloss. My thrilling white face was visible in the shine. Death makes mourning beauty that doesn't last absurd.

Tears of sweat mingled with the perfume on my

neck. I stared at myself in the mirror, closed my eyes, looked again. What am I supposed to do, open the fucking lid? Are they *easy* to open?

The Stink darted out from under the table and escaped. There was an insanely folded lined sheet of notebook paper lying on the coffin lid that I was trying not to look at. The scribbled writing had been done slowly with a blunt pencil.

To the other person in this Hoose:

I'm deed. I own the lot here. Don't think yoo'll get a ~~penny~~. Nuthin. My only son Neddie gets the lot. Fr Batchelor's on his waye. I've left word that yoo sleep like the devil. I always hated yoo even before what yoo done to an innocent beast. Don't think I don't know aw aboot yoo. Vengeance is Mine saith the Good Lord God in Heaven thy will be done.

Her son Neddie! It's beyond funny. *My* grandfather rumpy-pumpied that ugly old monster. The fruit of their union was a child molester.

And surprise, surprise: I, the deformer of her cat, am to be excluded from the spoils of her will. Uncle's inheritance is predictable vengeance. Surely she didn't think I'm stupid enough to imagine she'd give my house back to me?

I took the stairs two at a time, ran my bath, was in and out quick, put on my red Chinese dress and biker's boots, then went back down to the library. I sat in Napoleon's rocker by the unlit fire clutching my rosary.

She organised her death down to the last detail. Her timing was perfect. She polished her coffin, sprayed it with Blue Dew, climbed in and hauled down the lid then died. She even sent for Father Batchelor too late and cheated him out of his last opportunity to accuse her of mortal sin. She thinks of everything.

She's under that lid dressed for Hell, looking forward to damnation.

*

The Final Solution

Death is the only thing that interests me. This is the only place I'd die.

We're in the library, another fucking birthday Tuesday. Mother with her recently cracked Indian skin is passing round whisky toffees, Neddie the heir (my new stepfather!) is rocking himself in Napoleon's chair with orphaned Stinkie in his lap, stuffing his gaping hole and the cat's with stickies, licking his pudgy fingers, making a point of not staring at poor little lost Sam Dobson whose face is at his feet. A seven year old dying of demented trivia in a room full of ghouls.

I gave the butcher's boy a black jelly baby from my pocket. He didn't bite the head first. What a life he has in store. His father's a *butcher*, his mother's ugly as sin. Pearl prodded the little one in the gut.

'Say thank you,' she said, thrilled to be inside The Haugh at last. Mother only invited her so that she wouldn't be the oldest-looking middle-aged woman at Gorm's funeral.

The little one refused to look at me. He'll grow up into a butcher and ruin the family business.

Pearl said, 'I love your dress,' fingering the red chiffon with that well-known mix of envy and spite.

Her vermilion fingers smelled of bodily fluids. 'How much was it?'

The new bride stuck her head in between us shouting, 'More than she should be spending!' Her Indian cotton crinkle blouse brushed my sleeve.

'Some people are too thin,' she said prodding me in the gut. I beamed aggressive blue fizz right at her.

'The game's up now,' Neddie said, crashing into Napoleon's marble fireplace each time he rocked forward. When I looked at him he looked away.

His face has had that faraway smug expression since he informed me straight after Gorm's burial that he's sold The Haugh and all that's inside it. The new owner is taking possession immediately after the party. Nothing's to be touched.

None of it matters. They'll never force me out of here alive. That's not my destiny. Fate likes me again. My spiritual confidence is pure, clean, indestructible. Taking everything I want is easy. Nothing bad can happen ever again because I can't imagine it.

This feeling of power came as the old tyrant's body was secured in the vault this morning on the top of the pile. We were crammed into the mossy cave, heads bowed under the roof, listening to Father Batchelor pray for her soul when we heard the tide.

The mourners drifted towards the stairs preparing to lunge to safety. Father speeded up his chant, keeping an eye on the waves, asking God for, 'A wee delay please while we finish this important Rite.'

A white decisive alsatian bounded in, sniffed my gloved hand, barked at the coffin then disappeared along the beach.

As soon as Father shut his face everyone rushed the stairs. Alone at last I stuck my hand behind Great-grandfather's tomb. Sealed inside the spider's rose garden the pyschotically folded page says:

I am Donald Van Ness.
Anyone touches me
or my sister Sophira
will DIE.

The waves were closing in. On the back in black caps someone had added:

DEATH FOR BETRAYAL.

I ran up the stone steps to safety.

'Sophira looks much older than she is,' Mother was saying to Pearl. 'I was *extremely* young when the twins were born . . .' She looked at me sternly.

'It's very romantic,' Pearl gushed. 'Marrying two brothers.'

'Half-brothers,' Neddie said, reaching for another raspberry bun. Mother grabbed his hand and held it to her melons. Some people have no shame. The transparent skin of her eyelids cracked into a smile that made me long to die.

They insult my house just being in it.

Doctor Feathers said, 'Gorm knew her time was up,' attempting to press my wee white hand reassuringly. Cage the lawyer's son, giving me the glad eye, said, 'It was good of you to be with yer grannie at the end.'

He reminds me of somebody? A non-Jewish version of the Count! Younger, but just as ugly.

Father Batchelor cornered me in the hall.

'Death's fashionable,' he said, puffing his pipe. 'Everybody's doing it.'

He told me that joke at Napoleon's funeral.

Outside in the drive the new owner's Mercedes convertible is shaming the butcher's van, Father Batchelor's bike and the stupid wee orange car my mother and the pervert have bought to match their cardboard house in Glasgow. What a laugh.

The Haugh has always been mine. As if some idiot can just inherit it and sell it! Nothing can take it from me because I'd do anything to keep it. It's all I ever wanted.

Running through the forest towards the North Sea, my rosary thudding against my chest, the dog – Blondi – barking towards me, all seems possible. God gives us moments to resurrect for because without us he's nothing. Playing alone is no fun for Him.

He's standing on the sea wall in his SS uniform with his back to the drop, the famous lock of black hair blowing in the gale. His neck's white and clean. He has a spiritual glow. Evil looks innocent. His blood when it comes will be bright red.

His favourite weather starts, obscuring my

approach, but he must have seen me before exposing his vulnerable back to stare over the sea to eternity. One push and he'd shatter to dust like Donald.

His dog reaches me before I'm out of the trees. He pushes me onto the ground, devouring my face with his skinny red tongue. He's been expecting me.

Mad Jack Gray raises his hand in salute when Blondi and I run into the clearing. He has eyes in the back of his head. He knows everything. He is invulnerable, indestructible, immortalised in celluloid, forever Adolf.

Only I can destroy him now. He's the last victim. It's the final solution to everything.

But perfection can't be replaced. It's pathetic trying to obliterate it. And Jack, like Adolf, is immortal. He'd laugh if I slashed his throat.

He jumps off the wall, grabs my arm and pulls me through the trees, faster and faster, Blondi barking alongside. They run away from me, too far ahead for me to catch up.

'Come on,' Jack shouts.

He's almost at the house.

'Come see your birthday present.'

He's bought me The Haugh with the Count's money.

We evicted the last of the funeral guests, laughing at the look on Neddie's face when informed of my triumph.

Mother said, 'Misery has always come to the inhabitants of this house.'

I yawned in her face.

Jack stood apart, watching. His fringe had been allowed to fall into his eye. He's a dark horse. Only I can guess his dreams.

As they drove out of The Haugh for good we threw apples at their horrible orange car, then raced through the forest to our swing.

Jack pushed me, higher and higher, then sat on the wall, legs dangling, staring down into the crypt. He looks like a little boy.

We started walking along the beach. It was dark when we reached Storm.

Inside the Chapel Father Batchelor was slumped across the altar puffing white smoke. He muttered, 'You two are little devils . . . you're an unholy alliance,' then buried his face in his cassock.

I lit a candle. Jack stared out the broken window at the sky.

'Killing a priest,' he said, 'would be a disappointment – not a bit like murdering God.'

Walking home it turned cold. My chiffon sleeves
fluttered in the sea breeze. He draped his leather coat
round me. His eyes are different at night. They
remind me of the slasher.

The tide was coming in. My feet felt uneasy on the
sand. Jack whispered something impossible to hear
because of the waves. He smiles like an angel.

Blondi bounded along the beach to meet us, barking like a maniac. The three of us ran screaming,
beating the tide. It's our beach. We can do exactly
what we like on it.

Jack disappeared. I climbed up to the woods and stood
on the wall screaming his name through the trees.

Blondi appeared at the head of the stairs which
lead into the vault.

I climbed halfway down and whispered, 'Jack.'

The sea was already seeping in. It had covered the
first three steps at the bottom of the spiral.

No one else can die here now there's no room.

He shines his torch into my eyes. He's sitting with
The Stink on top of Gorm's tomb.

He promises the vault will not fill with water.

'Be brave,' he says. It's safe being up high.

Down in the space between the steps and his seat
on the tomb I can smell the black sea. He holds open
his arms. Donald will not let me fall.

I jump the gap. He leans longingly close and grazes my forehead with his teeth where the stigmata used to be.

We're rich and pure and indestructible.

'There are two things,' Donald told me, years ago, 'purity and money.'

The waves are swishing in, faster and faster, when The Stink slithers over the edge with a Splash! Jack jumps after him, wading in knee deep, exploiting his talent for death, holding the cat down with his boot, flicking open his razor, gesticulating exactly like beloved Adolf as he slashes its dead face. Blood sprays his cheeks like sweat.

He climbs back up beside me. I give him a black jelly baby. He bites the head off. He's the same as me. We sit watching the waves gash the dead cat against the rocks.

I know exactly what will happen next.

Every night at midnight we'll cross our beach to swim naked in the North Sea. Then run back through the trees to The Haugh and share the rocking chair by the fire, eating jelly babies. At daybreak we'll climb upstairs to the top of the house, jump on Grandfather's bed as long as we like, bathe in Blue Dew, then sleep like Heaven. We'll be insanely happy every day forever and ever.

Lies are easy to believe in but the truth sounds false.

DEAD GLAMOROUS

Carole Morin

'A dark bloodstained book fashioned from the motherlode of a bizarre upbringing'
Sunday Times

'A cocktail of sex, booze and film stars . . . It's hard to say what this novel is about, but the fast pace and punchy writing are addictive'
Guardian

'About five minutes after I finished this book I . . . started reading it again'
William Leith, *Mail on Sunday*

'Written with a tremendous *esprit*, urging the story along. Sparkles with quirky brilliance'
Maureen Cleave, *Daily Telegraph*

'A tantalisingly *noir*ish book which plays sophisticated games with truth and fiction'
Books of the Year, *Glasgow Herald*

'In *Dead Glamorous* heroin overleaps the Ewan McGregor cool débâcle and becomes something Morin can dismiss as an "excellent slimming aid" . . . Tomorrow will always be another outfit, reminiscent of a screen icon's moment'
New York Press

£6.99   0 575 40035 8

*IN*DI*GO*

BARREL FEVER

David Sedaris

David Sedaris's reading on National Public Radio made him one of US radio's most popular storytellers. With pitch-perfect sarcasm mingled with an underlying empathy, this collection of his best stories captures the essence of our secret preoccupations and delusions *Barrel Fever* is like a blind date with modern life, and anything can happen.

'A satirical brazenness that holds up next to Twain and Nathanael West'   *New Yorker*

'The full, unexpurgated "SantaLand Diaries" . . . are quite possibly the 31 funniest pages of text published in the last quarter-century. David Sedaris slays me'   *Seattle Weekly*

'Not every page of *Barrel Fever* will leave you laughing – thank goodness for the droll but manageable table of contents – but still, this is one of those "Open at your own risk" books . . . Wacky writing par excellence: original, acid and wild'   *Los Angeles Times*

'With a mordant wit akin to Evelyn Waugh's and the perceptive economy of William Trevor, Sedaris cross-pollinates humour and pathos to create some splendid, often emotionally disorienting moment . . . imagine Oprah with a sense of irony' *New York Newsday*

£6.99   0 575 40073 0

*IN*D*I*GO

Out of the blue...

INDIGO

the best in modern writing